I0708829

The Australian Pen Collection #4

HAUNTED HEARTS

Copyright © 2026 1231 Publishing
Cover and internal design © 2026 1231 Publishing
All authors retain copyright to their stories

All rights reserved.

No part of this book may be reproduced in any form—with the exception of brief quotations embodied in critical articles or reviews—without written permission from the publisher, 1231 Publishing.

The characters and events portrayed throughout this book are fictitious or are used fictitiously. Any similarity to real persons, living or dead, is purely coincidental and unintentional.

Paperback ISBN: 978-1-7637236-5-8
Digital ISBN: 978-1-7637236-9-6

1231Publishing.com

1231 Publishing
PO Box 77
Kallangur Q 4503
AUSTRALIA

Contents

Broken Locks. Broken Hearts

Jodie Lane

"Blasted tourists," Pierre Allard muttered, wrapping his gloved fingers around the bolt-cutters in the chilly Parisian air. At least there were no doe-eyed, lovelorn morons snapping new padlocks on the Pont des Arts this night. No doubt they were cosying up to each other in overpriced wine bars or embracing passionately in cramped apartments. He shivered guiltily at the thought of his own wife, Hortense, at home by herself. He'd told her the overtime was mandatory, not that he'd volunteered for it.

Pierre squeezed the bolt-cutters. The lock snapped

free, and he reached for it but fumbled. The padlock plummeted into the Seine with a swift splash.

"Putain!" he cursed. Then, "Mon Dieu!" as a shape shimmered up from the river and coalesced before him.

"No more," the apparition hissed. Livid eyes blazed hatred from a young woman's face. "No more false promises. No more locks."

Bolt-cutters raised in defence, Pierre gasped, "I'm taking them off! It's my job!"

The ghost demanded, "Where's your lover? Whose heart have you broken?"

Wide-eyed, Pierre pleaded. "No, you don't understand, it's my job!"

The icy breeze was nothing compared to her glare as she considered him. Finally, "No lover?"

Pierre coughed, wishing desperately someone would walk or jog past. "My wife is at home. She's expecting me at ten."

The ghost said nothing. Then she vanished.

Pierre was on bridge duty again. He approached the Pont des Arts cautiously, pushing his heavy-duty plastic cart from lock to lock as he snapped away, dumping the severed metal into the tub on top. Many had initials etched in them; others written in permanent marker.

He glanced around to make sure he was alone, then held his breath as, instead of binning one padlock, he tentatively dropped it over the edge.

The ghost flew up before him. "No more!" she

snarled. "No more false promises and broken hearts."

"Wait! It's me." Pierre swallowed hard. "I take the locks off."

She stared. "You again."

He could see the shimmering lights of the Louvre through her. She wore a summery dress—her bare arms clearly didn't feel the cold. The dress reminded him of one his wife had worn early in their marriage, over two decades ago.

"Who are you?" he asked.

The ghost narrowed her eyes. "Anais. Anais Dubois."

The silence stretched between them.

"Why are you here, Anais?" Pierre tried again. "Why do you hate the locks?" Now his initial fright had receded, he could see how young she was, or would have been. Barely twenty.

Her form wavered. "I'm waiting for my boyfriend," she declared, voice trembling. "We put a lock on this bridge. He said would meet me here."

What could he say to that? "How long have you been waiting?" he ventured at last.

She looked away.

"I'm terribly sorry," he murmured. "I don't think he's coming."

In a choked voice she replied, barely above a whisper, "I know."

In the distance, cars rumbled and beeped their way along the Champs-Élysées. Pierre's stomach chose that moment to rumble and his thoughts drifted to the dinner that would be waiting. A foil-covered casserole he didn't deserve.

"Why do you take the locks off?"

He jolted back to the moment. "It's my job. I work for the city. Cleaning graffiti off walls, picking up rubbish in parks. And this."

She considered him. "And yet they still come. Placing locks on the rails. Grand gestures of false love." Her lips curved in a cruel smile. "And you come along to cut it all off. Good."

A dog's bark made Pierre turn his head. When he looked back, the ghost was gone.

"Bonsoir." The dog owner's gruff voice came with a nod. Pierre managed a half-hearted response. The dog whined but walked on.

One month later, he snapped the first lock and sent it tumbling over the edge. Anais whooshed into being but stayed her angry accusations. "It's you," she said.

Pierre swallowed, gesturing to the new locks. "Do you think all of them are false?"

She wavered. "Perhaps." A longer pause. "Not all," she whispered.

"Perhaps... Perhaps they started true and over time fell out of love." Guilt gnawed at him. Thirty years was a long time.

Anais gazed at him. "Have you ever been in love?"

"Of course!"

"And?"

He hesitated. Distant laughter spilt from a party boat upstream. The Tour Eiffel sparkled, its light reflected off the low cloud cover onto the city of love.

"I met my wife, Hortense, not far from here. She and her friend were pasting flyers on a wall—for an environmental rally. I told them they couldn't, and they were hypocrites for polluting the city." He half-smiled at the memory. "She was so fierce. She stayed to argue even after her friend wanted to move on. I ended up helping them put up the rest of the flyers and having dinner with them."

"She sounds passionate." Anais' voice was curious.

"She was. She is." Pierre's eyes welled. "We just... we fell into a routine. Kids are grown up now." How could he complain about his dull life when this young woman had somehow been robbed of hers? Did she even know she was dead? "She's wonderful," he blurted. "Always leave me a hot plate when I'm out working late. She's got a temper but never holds a grudge."

The breeze shivered through Anais. Pierre coughed, then changed the subject. "How did you come to be here?"

Ghostly tears filled her eyes. "He wanted to break up. I asked him to meet me here to talk. He never came."

Pierre reached out to comfort her. His hand passed through her shoulder. "I'm sorry," he said awkwardly.

She stared at where he'd tried to touch her, gave him a mournful look, then faded.

He returned the next night, telling Hortense he'd been assigned extra shifts. One cut lock later, and

Anais materialised. She gazed at him quizzically.

"Would it... will it help once all the locks are gone?" He gestured to the bridge, weighed down with steel-snapped promises.

She considered. "I don't know. Perhaps. Is that why you keep coming back?"

He didn't know the answer to that.

"Tell me about your wife," she said.

So, he did. Every week he returned, summoned Anais' ghost and shared stories of Hortense. At first it was simple facts, but soon it became stories of their time together. His heart eased, and affection crept into his voice.

Adoration eventually coloured every word, even anecdotes marred with frustration and disagreement. Anais would laugh at the silly stories, sigh at how he bought flowers periodically because Hortense loved how they brightened the house, not because he needed to apologise for anything.

He also listened to the ghost as she told him all the things she'd loved about her boyfriend.

"We would fight over stupid things," she mourned. "But then he'd smile and I couldn't stay mad, and we'd go out for ice cream and then we'd have the same stupid argument the next day."

"Maybe you just weren't ready for each other," Pierre ventured. "You were young."

Such a waste of life. He still didn't know how she'd died, but given her passion, he had his suspicions.

When it came time for him to leave—always nine-thirty, or he'd miss his metro—Anais fell silent. She never tried to stop him, but she didn't wish him well either.

One evening he stayed late, even after the padlocks were all gone, packed into his cart. Early spring leached daylight into the sky much later, and pedestrians still frequented the bridge, but he parked his cart near a lamppost and Anais sat hugging her knees, mostly hidden from view as Pierre crouched down and pretended to work.

"Hortense and I are going away for a few weeks next month," he began. "She has family in Spain. When we get back, it won't get dark until very late. I won't see you until the days shorten again." He held his breath, waiting for her to cry, to rage.

She simply nodded.

When he returned, suntanned and chubby from enjoying too many tapas, he explained to his wife that he needed to go out one night. She understood.

On the Pont des Arts, long after midnight, Pierre pushed no cart, yet in his satchel he carried a pair of bolt cutters. Yet at the plop of a padlock into the river, Anais did not appear.

Only then did he notice the ghostly metal lying beside the lamppost where they'd last spoken. It shimmered and became more solid as he reached for it. His stomach sank as he read the two initials etched into it.

AD + PA, encircled by a heart.

"This cannot be," he muttered.

You would break my heart too? The words floated into his mind unbidden.

He held the lock in his hand and debated what to do. Snap the lock? Throw it into the river? Or keep it and risk Anais haunting him forever?

What would Hortense say?

He straightened as he closed his fist around the surprisingly warm metal. He glanced down, shocked at the heat. Opening his fingers, he saw the inscription had changed.

AD in the centre of a heart. Nothing else.

Tears leaked from Pierre's eyes as the padlock faded into nothingness, drifting away like mist on the river.

He went home to his love.

Plenty More Fish in the Sea

M A Maclean

"Let's go for a swim," Karl said. "It's a perfect day, and you look perfect in that bikini." He looked Alli up and down.

"I don't want to swim."

Alli stretched her legs out in the sun and wiggled her toes. Her smile broadened as she continued to gaze at them.

"But darling, this is an island resort, how can you resist a dip in the sea?"

Alli glanced up at Karl and back at her toes. "The water looks too cold. I'd much prefer to bask in the sun."

"We haven't swum together once." Karl wedged himself onto the sunlounger next to her. "We've danced, hiked, roller-skated, played tennis and mini golf."

"And bike riding. I loved that."

"We've had the finest food and wine."

"The crunchy snacks are my favourite."

Karl sighed. "We're having so much fun together. When I arrived here, I was alone and then I met you." He squeezed her hand. "I can't believe I didn't see you on the seaplane, but there you were on the beach that first evening."

"I was walking on the beach then," Alli said without taking her eyes off her toes. "Could we go bike riding again, instead of swimming? That would be gnarly."

"Gnarly." Karl laughed "Sometimes you sound like an old surf movie."

"A what? Oh yeah," said Alli, making a mental note to eavesdrop and gather a variety of contemporary superlatives from conversations around her.

Karl eased off the sunlounger and knelt on the sand. "I've only been with you a week, but it's been the best week of my life." He took Alli's hands in his, then turned her chin so she was looking at him instead of her toes. "Alli, I want you in my life, for more than just this holiday." Karl's words flowed out in an excited rush. "You could move in with me or if I'm rushing this, you could get a place of your own near mine to begin with. You said you work from home. We could make a life together. What do you say?" He kissed her salty lips.

She smiled at him, her eyes sparkled. "How about that swim now?"

"Well... okay. I know this is all sudden but you're so special." He swallowed and squeezed her hand. "There's no rush, just think about it."

"I hadn't expected this when I walked up the beach last week." She smiled as they walked across the sand. "Nothing like this has happened before."

"It sounds like you beguile men at the beach frequently."

"I come to the beach when circumstances allow." Alli stared out across the sparkling water. "I don't always meet men."

Karl laughed and kissed her hand. Alli held his hand tight and led him to the shoreline.

Waves rolled in and bubbled up their legs as they waded into the surf. They embraced as the water swirled and fizzed around them. "I know this sounds a bit corny." Karl twirled a tress of Alli's damp hair. "Our time together has changed me."

"Wanting to be here on the beach changed me too," said Alli.

"I know it's fast but could we?" Karl's words hitched. "Would you... be mine?"

Alli looked out towards the rocky outcrop offshore, then at the couples tangled together on the beach and finally, she looked into Karl's eyes. "Yes," said Alli. "In this perfect world, I could... be yours." She swayed, unsteady on her feet.

"You could? I'm so—"

"Race you to the rocks." Alli dived under a cresting wave and was gone.

"Wow, she can really swim fast." Karl watched Alli streak away. He dived into the next wave and chased after her. When he reached the deeper water at the back of the breakers he lost sight of her. This was not the romantic moment he thought it should be.

He swam hard to the rock outcrop and climbed out. Alli wasn't there. He scanned the water and that's when he saw her bikini bottoms bobbing towards the shore. His heart jolted. He swam to retrieve the spotted swim thing.

"Alli," he called as he spun in the water, searching. "Alli." Over and over, he dived and searched.

Desperate, he waved for the lifeguard. "Help. My girlfriend is missing."

The lifeguard and others joined the search. An hour later, the sun set. They dragged him, frantic and exhausted, back to the beach.

"We can't find her," said a voice in the near darkness.

"She said yes," Karl sobbed gripping the spotted bikini bottom.

"To what?" asked the lifeguard.

"She said she would go away with me."

"I said I could go away with you," said Alli to herself as she hid in a fold of rock out on the outcrop. Her fins glistened the moonlight, where a few hours there had been toes. "Well, in all my dry land days, that's never happened before. I could go away with him. I could take the extra strong, permanent catalyst, and keep my pretty toes, but I'd lose so much." She looked down at the pretty spotted bikini top Karl had bought her. "At least he has the bottoms as a souvenir, and the yes. I did say yes. He will remember that." She shrugged and flicked her fins.

"He'll find someone new. Don't they say there are plenty more fish in the sea?" She laughed. "And plenty more men on the beach."

Whispering Walls

J. H. Nelson

With my modest suitcase in hand, I thank the taxi driver and watch him drive away. There is no question, I have a huge fight ahead of me. My boss has faith in me—or he just wants me out of the office so he and his secretary can, well... you know how it goes.

The place looks worse than the photos suggested. Timber covers the windows, graffiti defaces its exterior. I can't begin to guess what lurks within the condemned hotel.

Construction fencing surrounds the property, so letting myself in is impossible. She is a grand old building. I try to see her closer, fenced in as she is, she resembles a prisoner, locked in and sentenced to death. My heart aches at the thought. I need to get inside.

A trip to the council's office, a few sneaky lies and two popped buttons later, I have the keys and try to hide my enthusiasm while racing towards my target.

Darkness reigns in the boarded-up building, hindering my first glimpses inside. I pull out my phone and activate its torch. The smell of decades-old stale beer lingers. Floorboards creak beneath my feet as they're disturbed for the first time in probably years. The thought saddens me as I imagine her rich character back in the day. Music and cigarette smoke swirling up towards the rooms above, while men laugh together over a pint at the bar, discussing life and swapping stories. My mind returns to the reality before me, and I sigh.

Spray paint covers walls and I spot evidence of squatters by an old mattress and some ancient takeaway boxes.

What stories would you tell if you could talk? What sights have your walls seen within and without? Gosh, what I'd give to hear them.

"You weren't invited. You aren't welcome here. Leave!"

With a thud, my phone hits the floor. I spin around, looking for the person behind the creepy whisper. This isn't the first time I've come up against angry investors wanting me... out of their way.

"Who's there?" I retrieve my phone, its torch still activated. No one. Cautiously, I continue my walk through the majestic building.

"Why have you come? Please leave!"

Clinging to my phone this time, I still struggle to locate the owner of the disgruntled voice.

"Who's there? I mean no trouble." Not entirely true, but as a thirty-year-old woman, I have a better chance of defusing an altercation rather than winning any physical fight. "I'm Ada. I'd love to hear what you know about the hotel. Did you know the hotel back when she was trading?" I listen intently. Footsteps, floorboards, fabric rubbing against itself, anything... but there is only the sound of my breathing.

Goosebumps rise along my arms, the hairs standing on end. What if the voice I'm hearing isn't a person? Well... not one with a pulse. I hear a gasp and spin around with dizzying speed before realising it was mine. I take a few steadying breaths. My phone, still tightly in hand.

"I want you to leave! People are not welcome here!"

"What's your name? Were you the keeper of the hotel? Are you stuck here?" Part of my brain—the logical, more rational part—thinks I must've left my last marble stuffed in my suitcase back at the Motor Inn. Another part, however, knows that I'm right. That this is real and I'm not crazy. Which, in itself, has me questioning my sanity. "Please, I just want to talk to you about the hotel. I'm a historian. I fight for important heritage buildings and landmarks to remain standing, and I'm here to fight for this one. Will you help me save your hotel? Will you talk to me?" My question echoes through the empty building and I wait, my stomach in my throat and my breath held.

"I can't trust you. You're just like all the others. Everyone wants my land. My space. They want to destroy the hotel. Well, I will not let them. If you truly mean no harm, then leave." The boarded windows somehow rattle. A warning.

"Okay. I'll go. But I'll be back tomorrow. I want to talk. I need to learn everything I can about the hotel in order to save it. And you can either help me or not, but either way, I'm going to protect this precious building. Your beautiful home! I really hope you'll help me. The council's going to put up an ugly fight without it."

Back in my modest motel room, I get straight to work researching every article I can find on the Kelpie Creek Grand Hotel. I find myself paying particular attention to anything relating to any of her proprietors, publicans or landlords who have come and gone throughout her successful years. It is midnight when I close the laptop and crawl into bed.

It is still early when I head into the hotel armed with a sandwich, my laptop, notepad and pens. A woman can never be too prepared when she's hoping for answers from a newfound ghost friend— hopefully he's feeling more cooperative today.

Stepping across the threshold, I listen for any signs of my untrusting counterpart. Nothing. I frown, understanding he may not come or make himself known. Not one to shy away from a challenge, I switch tactics.

"Good morning. Is anyone here?"

Once again, nothing.

I make my way upstairs to where our conversation took place and hope he's there. No success there, either. A new idea sparks, putting a smirk on my lips.

"Well, looks like I have the whole place to myself for the day to do my research."

"I told you, you're not welcome here!"

"Aha! I knew you were here!" As I chuckle, I hear something resembling a whispered sigh, and I smile, proud of my ingenuity. "So, are you ready to help me save your hotel?"

Together we run through everything from the building's first day of construction, its wartime use as a makeshift hospital, to the surprising discovery that it also served as a boarding school for outreach farmers for many years. Nibbling on my sandwich, I madly scrawl notes and dates on my page.

"So... wait. Are you saying that she was one of the original buildings? That the township wasn't established beforehand?"

"She? Who is she?"

"Sorry. The hotel itself. I tend to call them 'she.' It never seems right to think of them as an 'it'. To me, they are so much more than that."

"I don't appreciate being called a 'she'. Can you not feel my masculine energy? My dominant, authoritative ambience?" The last word, a harshly accentuated hiss.

I flinch at the intended intimidation. Refusing to budge, however, I replay his words. Study them in my mind. They don't make sense. 'I don't appreciate being called a 'she'. Can you not feel my masculine energy? My ambience?'

"Oh my god," I whisper as understanding dawns. "You're not the publican. You're… you are the…" The words stick in my throat as I process what this means.

"You thought I was a what? A ghost? Hardly. Humans have used me since the rise of my walls, but never for more than their own benefit. They are selfish creatures who take what is not theirs and destroy whatever stands in their way. Humans, alive or passed, aren't welcome here."

Sitting cross-legged with my back against the wall, I feel it for the first time. A heaviness hits me in the heart. The sadness behind his words runs deep. He's been let down by people, leaving him cynical and untrusting.

Twisting, I close my eyes and hold my palms against the timber wall. "I'm so sorry that people have hurt you. You didn't deserve that. If you'll let me… If you'll open your heart just one more time, I promise I'm going to do everything I can to save you. I don't want you to hurt anymore. I want to feel the happiness that I know you once held."

A tear rolls down my cheek.

Rushing through the street under the bright sun, sweat beads along my brow, but nothing can slow me down. Scanning for prying eyes, I duck through the hole in the fence and let myself into the hotel.

"We did it! We won the appeal! First step down. Now we have one month to convince them of all the reasons why you're so special." A warm rush touches my skin. It moves like a palpable shift of energy. The whisper of something akin to embarrassment vibrates in the air surrounding me. After a moment to process what's happening, I register that it's not my feelings I'm experiencing. "Are you embarrassed? Why?" I ask.

He remains silent, but the feeling stirs again, making my heart swell. I suddenly wonder to myself how it all works. Does he feel my energy the same way I'm learning to feel his? Can he see me? Or only hear me? Too self-conscious to voice my thoughts, I refocus on my work, but not before discerning the heat radiating from my cheeks.

"So, how are we going to convince the board of your accentuated charms without demonstrating your... sentient side?" I pace the floor in thought.

The floor beneath me morphs, moulding me into a highly perched seat that lifts my feet well off the floor. His voice echoes around me. "You're giving me a headache."

"Um... What? You can... move?!" The idea that I've gone completely mad crosses my mind. How else does one bend the notion of logic to this degree, without the rational concept of mental health being a factor?

"You're not crazy." I detect his sigh. Somehow, I

know he's rolling his eyes at my naivety—or is it my very human-ness—he's laughing at?

"Hey... give me a minute to catch up, okay? It isn't every day a girl meets a sentient hotel," I retort, feeling stupid and inferior in his presence. "Wait. Did you guess that, or did you hear my thoughts? How do your abilities work?"

Amusement swirls around me.

"Please don't laugh at me. You've had a lifetime to grow into and accept your gifts. I am on the back foot and asking you to help me understand. I want to know you... properly."

The space fills with remorse and a gentle understanding. "You're right. I'm sorry." The warmth of a caress envelopes me and calms my vulnerabilities. "Okay... I can hear you. I sense all that you feel and can detect undercurrents of your vibrations... your intentions, some might call it. I know it is you before you enter, for instance. My sense of smell is strong actually, so yes, I can smell you. This is also why I prefer not to have flowers inside."

"No flowers. Noted. Can you see me? Oh god... wait. Does that mean you can smell my feet?" I ask in horror.

He chuckles. "I like your scent. You remind me of sweet peaches. Fresh. Lovely."

A heated blush hits me, but I can't tell if it's his or mine. Awkwardly, I jump into more questions.

"Can you see me?"

He pauses. "I can see you, but in my experience,

it's different from how you do. I feel like humans see in… sharp lines, yes? My sight is not like that. Mine is soft. Blurry. I must work very hard to see detail."

"Oh." I absorb his words. "Well, I'll stop worrying when I have a pimple or wake up with bed hair—" the words are out of my mouth before I realise what I've said. "Oh… not that I was planning on you seeing my bed hair. I'm not staying overnight… that wasn't… you know… that wasn't what I meant. I wasn't trying to—"

"It is very late," he yawns. "You'll stay here tonight. No-goods roam the street at night."

Looking at my watch, I'm shocked by the time. The idea of walking back to the Inn doesn't thrill me, but I'm not equipped to spend the night here, either. I am not sleeping on that squatters' mattress downstairs.

"Don't even think about it. I can feel your thoughts, remember? I'm not letting you go. I can't protect you from the no-goods out there. Here, I can keep you safe. Please? I'd really like you to stay."

Shyness creeps to me along with a rush of heat. An undercurrent of something else lurks behind the shyness, but he blocks it before I get a read on it. When I accept, his beautiful worn timber moulds to my body perfectly. I never imagined that a hard surface could be so comfortable.

He pulls me close, embracing me like a mother cradles her infant. I lean into the feeling, enjoying the safety of his protective presence. A blanket drapes across me. I don't know where he got it from but it smells clean and I snuggle into it as slumber calls.

My body warms quickly under the weight of the quilt, and it isn't long before I'm peeling it off. That's when I recognise that he is anything but sleepy. Giddiness crowds the air around me, sparking an equal fire of my own. Reading my enthusiasm, his excitement doubles.

Unsure of what I'm doing or how to broach the subject with him, nervousness overtakes all of my senses. An odd-shaped timber beam moves towards me, extended like a human arm—is that the staircase banister? With it, he drags my fringe away from my eyes and I experience how hard he is concentrating to see me closely. "Do you trust me?"

A heady mixture of tenderness and ardent desire surrounds us. A passionate storm builds and my fears melt away. I surrender to the yearning I can no longer deny. "With all that I am."

With only two weeks before the council makes its final decision on the fate of the hotel, we draft our proposal to turn the hotel into a town museum. As the oldest building in Kelpie Creek, it makes sense that it should house and highlight the thick history of the town's tragedies and triumphs.

"And you will stay here with me? You can run tours by day. I can add ambience to your stories and then by night... we can... be together."

The uncertainty and vulnerability rolling off his aura almost breaks me. I throw all of my intention and love behind my words. "There is no other place on this earth I want to be. You are my other half. My person—except you aren't a person—so I guess I will call you my... soul? No. My love. Yes. You are my beautiful, gentle-souled love."

Affection gushes all around me. I observe a flicker of embarrassment amidst the air, but absorb it silently and project all my love back.

Overwhelmed and shaking, I stare at the council's 'letter of demolition order' in my hand. The fate of our future sealed within makes my stomach queasy.

"Open it, my love. We'll need to open it sometime. Let's get it over with and what will be, will be."

I hear his words, but I know he's as scared as I am. I tear open the envelope, my heart racing and my palms sweaty.

DEMOLITION ORDER DENIED

This letter hereby states and supports the repair and restoration of the Kelpie Creek Grand Hotel for the purpose of a Town Memorial Museum. The overseer has 90 days to commence works on the property or the land will be forfeited and re-titled into the name of the council's bidding.

Reading the last paragraph, tears swell and fall from my eyes like a dam being released. We won?

"Oh my god... we won!" I jump around like a lunatic. One very happy lunatic. The fright of my life comes from a deafening boom. Light floods the hotel. Unable to hold his joy, my beautiful hotel has blown the boards off his windows.

Together, we pause and silently soak up the joy and love emanating between us. No longer fearful of what our future holds, we unlock the last depths of our hearts to each other in a soundless embrace of pure emotion. Together forever. We are... home.

Kitsune's Tale

Nyssa Baschel

"Foxgloves!" Reihime shouted as she grabbed a bouquet from the restaurant table and shoved it at my lace blouse, the blouse I bought especially for *her* wedding.

I wiped off the pollen with that same miserable sensation that followed me wherever I went. No matter what I did, I didn't fit in. "They're not *that* bad."

"Not bad?" She yelled above the rowdy guests arriving from Saint Patrick's Church up the street. "Not bad? They might do for *your* wedding, if you ever have one, but *I* ordered roses – cream roses."

I didn't bother arguing, Reihime had her expectations. That's the sister she is.

I glanced over at the Irish bar bearing a myriad of spirits against the warm stone wall. The hearth was generously decorated with, God forbid, foxgloves. *Gráinne Uaile*, was what they called the restaurant, something about a pirate queen from Connacht. Perfect for Reihime.

"Talking about weddings," her tone changed like the wind, "I want you to meet Aaden." My sister threw a wave over the gathering crowd, catching the attention of an Irish man in a tweed hat and jacket. His fair cheeks were bloodshot and his teeth crooked.

"Reihime," I whispered in my sister's ear, "I'm not here for this, I'm not even over the jet lag."

"Oh, stop being such a stick-in-the-mud and embrace the moment for once in your life. You're in the Emerald Isles, the most romantic place on Earth."

"Reihime—" I hardly got the word out before the brawny man arrived in front of us.

"This is my very single sister, Kit," Reihime beamed, pulling me closer. "Kit... Aaden, a local farmer from here in Newport."

His grin extended from ear to ear. "Is that like Kit-Kat?"

"No," I said, "It's Kitsune, meaning a Japanese fox spirit."

He snorted a laugh. "Nothing like that vermin hidin' in the backfield killing my chickens, I'm sure."

"Foxes aren't vermin," I defended, "they are just

messengers, misunderstood."

"This one is vermin. It's managed to avert every trap I've set." He cleared his throat. "But of course, of course. So, what are two beautiful Japanese women doing in the likes of Mayo?"

I glanced towards the band setting up, my way of saying I'm not interested.

"We're not really Japanese," Reihime chimed in, "well, our mother is, but our father's Irish. We were brought up in Peggy's Cove, Nova Scotia."

I shot her a burning glare. I didn't want this man knowing anything about me. Nothing important, anyway.

"Excuse me." I didn't wait for permission, I swiftly wove through Reihime's friends, mostly Canadians, and stole through the front door.

Night turned the cloudy sky into a darker shade of grey, and misty rain speckled the tables. I glanced over my shoulder to see Aaden excuse himself from Reihime and shuffle towards the door. I bit my bottom lip; he obviously didn't take the message. Unlike Reihime, I wasn't about to throw away my life to some arsehole who couldn't take his eyes off other women. It made me sick to watch Reihime making all the same mistakes as our mother. That wouldn't be my life. My life is full, perfect. I have a sought after marketing job waiting for me in Toronto for the *Soul Shine Magazine*, and a wonderful network of friends. The last thing I needed was some man holding me back—or at least that's what I told myself.

I threw one last glance back and slipped down the

narrow lane. The ocean wind cut through my blouse as I struggled to keep my heels from catching in the cracks between the cobblestones. Hawthorn clutched at my clothes.

"Kit-Kat," Aaden yelled behind me, "are you out here?"

Goosebumps broke out across my arms. Was he stalking me? I sprinted around the back of the restaurant. Then I heard a cackle and a strange gekkering sound and my eyes darted towards the bins and crates.

A fox.

"Kit," Aaden called, closer.

My heart jumped. "You can't be here," I whispered to the fox, "he'll kill you." But the creature slinked closer, nose in the air as if inviting me to play. "Go!" I said sternly.

Aaden's footsteps closed in. "I know you're here."

Damn, I raced towards the fox to chase it away, but it dived in a circle as if leaping in a field.

"Shoo," I whispered forcefully.

"Kit-Kat."

Cackle. Cackle.

I grabbed the fox, earning myself a yelp, and darted under the backstairs. Sodden grass soaked through my skirt, and the fox's black paws sullied my blouse. I released a shallow sigh. I couldn't go back to Reihime's wedding like this.

Aaden's feet passed by before I released the fox and hurried towards my rental car. Reihime would kill me but I would have to wear something shockingly inappropriate from my suitcase. I'd have to be quick.

I slipped the key in the ignition, when out of the corner of my eye I saw Aaden. My skin crawled, he was making for his car.

"You're joking," I whispered, and ripped out of the car park. Heart in my throat, I sped towards my Airbnb outside of town. The moon cast her silvery light across stone walls and the island littered harbour. Beech trees arched overhead, shadows danced across the narrow lanes.

I put my foot to the pedal, Reihime would never forgive me if I missed her wedding reception.

Suddenly, something red darted in front of my car. I hit the brakes and the tyres screeched across the waterlogged road. My heart raced as I gripped the steering wheel. Hawthorn flashed past the windows.

The world spun.

The last thought I had was '*oh shit, this is going to cost me a fortune.*' Then everything went black.

"Nine tales. Kitsune has nine tails, one for every life of hard-won wisdom." That was what my mother used to tell me in the long evenings before Da shuffled home drunk before dawn. Tears would gleam in her dark eyes. "We make our bed, Kit, we lie in it. This is the wisdom my mother once told me." But that was a long time ago, before moving to Canada, and Japan became nothing more than a memory.

My mother's sad smile faded amidst twisted

branches, too bright for the dark. My head throbbed. Then a twig broke and I jumped, shooting a glare into the darkness. The seatbelt cut into my shoulder and I wiped aside my black hair only to see my hand covered with blood – my blood.

"Ya alright, lass?" A man's voice asked in a heavy Irish accent.

I stared up at him through the window. Something about him didn't make sense. His bright red hair brushed over his prominent brow, his sculptured cheeks framed his piercing green eyes. I swore he must have been the most gorgeous man on earth.

And there I was, trapped in a car, bleeding all over the steering wheel.

"Wait a moment," his baritone voice had a reassuring ring. He tried to yank the door open but it refused to give. He stopped for a moment, and then with a playful grin, he held up a finger like he had an idea. I closed my aching eyes, and faded in and out with wooziness.

The door groaned and cracked open, and the most gorgeous man on earth dragged me from the twisted wreck. I struggled to find balance, my legs weak.

He threw my arm over his broad shoulder. "My house isn't far from here," he said, "Ya welcome to stay if ya like."

Half dazed, I nodded. "What's your name?"

"Tadhg," he smiled a bright, beautiful smile. His forest green eyes twinkled as we shuffled through the moon-soaked woods.

"Tie-g," I said. "I like that."

"It means storyteller or poet, some would even say philosopher, but in truth, d'ey all mean d'e same. Ya see?"

I didn't dare look into his inviting stare, it would only get me into trouble. "My name's Kit, Kitsune."

I sensed more than saw his boyish grin. "*Fox spirit*," he said softly.

At that I turned to him. "How do you know?"

"I told ya, I'm a storyteller. I know everything."

I studied his fair chiselled face, and in that moment I almost believed him. "How far's your home?"

"We're here."

I looked through the light-drenched bushes and my jaw dropped; the house had appeared out of nowhere. A mansion, three stories high, with generous bay-windows and stylish wooden beams

"Come on," he said, "let me make ya tea, and light us a fire in the hearth."

I let him help me to the grand door. I didn't even see him open it as we walked into a lounge room of velvet and dark wood furniture. I sat on the couch and lowered my head as the hearth flared to life under his capable guidance. Then he knelt before me, a warm cloth wiping away the blood and grit from my face. His crimson hair flickered with the flames.

"Thank you," I mouthed.

This time, he didn't smile. He leant forward and sank his soft lips over mine. My body set alight, tingling with a yearning I didn't know I had until that moment. It was insane. I wanted him more than I ever wanted anything.

Actually, this *was* crazy, this wasn't me.

"I'm sorry," I said, "I don't know what came over me."

But there was no shame in his stare, only a playful dance that promised a challenge.

Suddenly, I was acutely aware that I was alone with him in the countryside, and I didn't even have my phone.

I pushed him away, but somehow he slipped through my defences and pulled me closer.

"I have a story for you – Kitsune, spirit of the fox." His kisses gently found their way down my neck, and he slipped my blouse from my shoulders with hands too nimble to be human. "There was once a white queen who came upon barren fields of rice. She whispered her name and impregnated the water-bound crops. She saved them all – the starving, impoverished, and dying under the Emperor's cruel regime." His kisses sank deeper, and his hands brushed across my naked back. "And when she left, she blessed them with her children, messengers of another world."

"What was her name?" My breath slowed, and deepened.

"She has nine tails, I should know, after all she is my queen—"

My eyes flashed open, I knew this story. My mother had told it to me a thousand times. The tale always ended the same – *"Kitsune will not save us. We make our bed, Kit, we lie in it."*

Maybe that was why she named me that, she still had hope when she had her first born daughter. In haste, I pulled up my blouse. "I have to go."

"Before you leave, consider this," he whispered, "if you know her name then you don't belong in this world. Come with me." But Tadhg didn't stop me, he simply let me go. I raced towards the door, buttoning up my blouse, and out into the moonlit night.

The last thing I heard him say was, *"Regret is a woeful beverage, fox spirit, a slow poison."*

It was days before I made my way back to the car that was somehow wedged between a tree and the stone wall. I circled the wreckage. God only knows how Tadhg got me out, how I survived.

"This is just like you," Reihime said, casually stepping around the wreckage. "You are a walking disaster. You've ruined everything – including my wedding and our hire car credit rating. It's like mother said, you don't belong in this world."

I felt the thrum of my pulse in my neck. I was never going to live this down. "She says I'm not *of* this world, not that I don't *belong* in this world – there's a difference." But I couldn't help recalling what Tadhg said.

"I can't see a difference." Reihime walked on.

My ache in my heart ached for Tadhg with every day that passed. It was madness really, everything my mother warned me against, but I longed for his stories, the way he understood me, his gentle lips exploring the valleys of my neck. My plan was simple;

I would search these woodlands for his mansion and give him some feeble apology for why he might consider me back into his life.

"Look," I turned back to Reihime, "I'll go it alone from here."

Before she could chastise me for being harebrained for not following the well-trodden path of marriage and motherhood, I disappeared into the birches and oaks. Tadhg was a man, of course, but he was different somehow. It didn't feel like he would whisk me away to an unknown land and demand I wait on him hand and foot, while he was out flirting with half the town.

I walked for hours, over fallen logs, through stinging nettles and around lichen covered rocks, but the mansion was nowhere to be seen. I stopped near the road, hands on my hips as I caught my breath.

"Aye lass," an old man called from down the lane. "Ya lost, are ya?"

"No," I said as he shuffled up to me in a ragged jumper, jeans and wellies. "I'm looking for a man, Tadhg. He owns a mansion around here."

The man's brow creased. "Tadhg, ya say?" He fingered his chin. "No, I can't say I know him, and I've lived here since I was a wee boy."

"What?" I glanced back towards the trees, how could that be?

"There's a mansion though."

I spun back towards him. "There is?"

"Sure, I'll take ya there."

My hope reignited, I said, "Thank you, I appreciate

this."

I shadowed him, back through the dense woods. Ivy crept over the trail, making it almost indiscernible. The man mumbled about the town and how many avoided this forest, most which I missed thanks to his heavy accent.

We came to a clearing; sunlight streamed down from the prodigious sun through the clouds. My heart stopped, my mouth ajar. There in front of me was an old abandoned mansion. Tree branches poked through the weathered, half broken roof. There was no glass in the bay-windows. I would have told him this was the wrong house, only it was shaped exactly like the one Tadhg led me to in the dead of night.

Vaguely, I heard the old man mutter, "I don't think anyone's lived here for a very long time."

Experimental World

Margaret Dakin

Frank hadn't been able to visit his hidden laboratory for almost a week. He'd been obliged to attend a scientific conference in Canberra that had been arranged by his workplace supervisor at the Research Centre which was attached to the Brisbane Planetarium.

He'd gone down to the Capital reluctantly. Frank worked partly from home, his contract stating that he wasn't required to use his work hours in the same manner as his colleagues at the Research Centre, provided he contributed an equivalent amount of progress to whatever enterprise the group was investigating at the time. They had been tracking the sun and the planets, and conducting trials into counteracting the problems humankind was experiencing. The conjecture was that these would be exacerbated in the future by pollutants in the air and oceans, global warming, and the increasing world population. He liked his role at the Centre, though he had an additional project at home, and he knew that lately he'd been a bit absent-minded; and probably that was why his boss had insisted he go to Canberra.

While away, he'd kept to himself in the evenings, his faithful companion a glass of whisky, sipped slowly in his hotel room as he read his notes from the day's conclave. He didn't need much sleep; thoughts of his private research providing a constant distraction and making him eager for the think-tank in Canberra to end.

His pet theory, indeed the postulation on which he'd based most of his experiments, continued to be that the earth's sun is less than halfway through its lifespan, and that six billion years from now, it would probably not be Homo Sapiens who would watch the sun's demise. As it had taken nearly four billion years of natural selection for bacteria to become the human genus they were today, Frank believed they'd continue to develop. He'd decided it would be important to make sure they proceeded in a direction which could allow the dominant species to exist on a planet with rising seas and increasingly denuded resources. He surmised that eventually, any inhabitants that had evolved, would find it necessary to shoot off to another galaxy.

Now thankfully back home, Frank dumped his luggage on the kitchen table and immediately rolled aside the carpet square on his lounge room floor. He heaved up the wooden hatch that provided access to his underground laboratory, anxious to again greet his friends.

Over the years, through hard physical labour, he'd created a very sophisticated set-up beneath his house. He'd installed solar power, and it was irrigated by seepage from a subterranean layer of water-bearing permeable rock, which he pumped into buried tanks. He always knew that fate had led him to this secluded property in the hinterland behind Brisbane, and when he'd discovered this natural aquifer, he'd seemed destined to continue his experiments here.

Looking down, the dim light from the solar batteries reassured him that all had continued as it should while he was away. Nevertheless, he felt there was something that was not quite right, and it was with a touch of apprehension that he activated the bank of bright lights over his work bench, then edged down the steep cement steps. He'd expected the smell to be bad when he got back, but the stench that now caused him to put his hand over his mouth and pinch closed his nostrils, was deadly.

As usual he was eager to see what progress his most successful embryos had made. There lurked an element of ethical criminality in his experiments of course, because officially he'd destroyed the eggs on which he'd been conducting trials into a cure for a wide range of diseases. However, when he'd concluded that original assignment, he'd not been able to resist further tests on the microcosms he'd seen growing under his microscope.

His own secret passion had always been in creating hybrids. This involved cross fertilization of animal eggs and human sperm. He'd also developed cybrids in which a human nucleus was implanted into an animal cell. He thought these experiments might be useful in the future.

For a moment, despite his disquiet at the odour, Frank could not help gloating at the invisibility of his laboratory. As Dr Frank Von Stein, acknowledged as a brilliant lateral-thinking scientist, he commanded the respect of his colleagues. His eccentric habits and solitary lifestyle inevitably resulted in his gradually becoming a figure of ridicule, though this had not been done in an overt manner. He knew by what name his fellow scientists referred to him behind his back, and he was amused that the joke was on them. His secret project had been successful.

It had taken several years, but the eggs which had commenced as no more than a wriggle under his microscope, had now become living creatures, the like of which no other human had seen. No one could imagine what lurked in this covert workshop under his house.

He'd not known what to expect when he'd first

began his exploration. Along the way there had occurred many misadventures which he'd carefully disposed of in the incinerator in his backyard. Although each step had been meticulously documented in the score of journals he kept under his bench, he still didn't quite understand the chain of circumstances that had finally led him to produce these remarkable off-spring, the family for which he'd always longed. No longer the dispassionate scientist, he was protective of them, and despite their immunity to all current diseases, he determined to keep them isolated for as long as possible before exposing them to the curiosity and exploitation of the outside world.

'She' looked beautiful. He considered her to be female due to her being a hybrid produced from an Echidna egg that had been fertilized by human sperm. He'd named her Clare. Instead of spines, her body had produced pale silky hair. As she'd never been obliged to ferret deep into the earth for ants, her nose had not grown long and pointed, but was small and rounded. Her hind legs were short but shapely, and her forelegs ended in five digits and delicate nails, with which she handled her food in a dainty manner.

'He' was the product of a human nucleus implanted into the cell of another resilient native, a male dingo. He also was covered in hair, but reddish and coarser than Clare's. He walked on his hind legs, possessed powerful forearms, and although his teeth had grown long and sharp, his face appeared more human than canine. Frank called him Dante, after the author of his favourite poem.

The carbon footprint of the pair was slight, as they ate a meagre diet of raw vegetables laced with vitamins to compensate for the fact that they were confined in a sunless place. They digested their food with no gasses escaping from their bodies, and drank only water. Keeping themselves clean, they seemed indifferent to fluctuations in temperature, needing no artificial heating or cooling system in the underground room where they lived.

He'd been careful to leave his children adequate food for the time he'd expected to be in Canberra, and the drip feed system would have provided them with clean water. Now, before he renewed their supply of sustenance, he was anxious to clear the odour from the confined space, which despite the constant in-ducting of fresh air, was making him sick.

He still thought of these creatures as his children, though they now both had become stronger and, in the case of Dante, almost as tall as he was. Although pleased with the progress of the experiment, his one regret remained that he'd not been able to invoke in them any human traits such as speech. Although he had a deep affection for them, he felt let down by their inability to return his devotion.

Now, apprehensive and trying not to breathe deeply, Frank took a handkerchief from his pocket and tied it over his nose. He reached for the pressurised hose which he used to sluice out the cages. But when he picked up the hose, barely a dribble came from the nozzle.

Frank hurried to Clare's enclosure and found her huddled in the corner, eyes shut and her tongue hanging out. He was alarmed when he noticed that her water trough was bone dry. Also he saw that the bars on her cage had been bent. He knew she couldn't have summoned the strength to do that, even though she must have been desperate for water.

Horrified, he realised she was dead, probably had been for at least twenty-four hours, and that was mostly the reason for the stench in the room.

He turned to the other pen and observed that the bars on it were similarly bent. There remained a little water in that trough, but other than the pile of excreta around the waste hole in the corner, the cage was empty. He pulled from his belt the stun-gun he always armed himself with when he came down to the laboratory.

Suddenly, he detected warm breath on his neck and heard a low growl. He turned. Dante stood just behind him. Dropping the hose, Frank fired as the male lunged at him. They went down together, and he experienced sharp teeth digging into his neck as the powerful jaws ripped at his jugular.

Frank struggled up and leant against the wall. He saw Dante, apparently unaffected by the dart which protruded from his cheek, lumber into Clare's cage and take the beautiful body in his arms. Even as Frank experienced his own life ebbing away, his emotions were mixed.

There was grief he would no longer be conducting his research, and fear for the fate of these loved ones.

However, there was also an undercurrent of triumph, as he saw the human tears running down Dante's face and heard him crooning sadly, again and again, the word "Clare", as he slowly rocked her back and forth.

Ella

Ryan Alcock

"You know he's a vampire, right?"

Err, no. Of course not. I mean, sure he's tall, saturnine, moody and probably sexy if you like that sort of thing, but I don't, and just because he's wearing a velvet vest and pirate shirt, doesn't automatically suggest that Miss is a vampire (it's short for Amis, which I'd like to point out isn't actually shorter, but supposedly I'm missing the point).

He's dancing with Ella Foster, who is my best friend, and who, if I'm honest, I'm probably a little bit in love with. She pretends she's stupid, but she's very funny. And, she's gorgeous, and I mean *gorgeous*. She has a figure to die for, long light brown hair, and dark eyes that are *so* dark. Also, an absolutely cute-as nose. And a smile to die for. And she does this thing with her tongue where she sort of touches the side of her lips and...

Okay, so, a lot in love with.

We've been best friends since we were ten, and at fifteen I realised I was totally in love with her, and that led to three high school years that were *really* tough. I went away for three months only to come back to find she's dating this guy called Amis "Miss" Wakelin. I mean, credit to the guy for claiming Miss as a nickname. If I didn't hate him on principle, I'd admire him. Well, that and the fact, apparently, he's a vampire, as I've been informed by Chibi (whose real name is Belle Livingstone, and she tells me we've been at school together for our senior years, but I can't remember any Belle or Chibi or whatever).

Miss is dancing with Ella and some other chick who, since I've got back, no one has been able to identify. Ella made some comment about her being Miss' sister, but honestly, I've seen them by themselves, and they are *super* close for siblings. Like... creepily close.

"Do you know who that girl is?" I ask Chibi.

"Oh, that's Valentina," Chibi says glibly.

"His sister?"

"Oh God, no," Chibi giggles, and it's that weird childish giggle which might explain why we weren't friends in high school. "Valentina is to Miss what you are to Ella," and for the first time that night, I'm thrown off guard by my new friend.

"What's that supposed to mean?"

"A puppy following her master. Or mistress." She looks at me, and there's almost delight in her cruelty. I want to defend myself, but earlier I poured my heart out to Chibi and so she knows the truth. Using it against me just seems harsh. I do that thing where I turn to study something, but truthfully, I'm just hoping the tears don't run down my cheeks.

Chibi found me when I was having a sob about the harshness of life and the cruelty of love, and she was really nice – I thought.

Composure restored, I turn back to her and zero in on what I'm most curious about.

"So, Valentina loves Miss?"

"Oh, babe, they're married."

Wait, what?

"Okay, so here's the thing, vampires are a bit like Mormons," Chibi says.

"That's probably really offensive," I object.

"Dude, are you a Mormon?"

"I'm not sure that's the point."

"No, the point is that vampires have more than one bride. If she's not one already, Ella will be his second one. Valentina is his first." I search the net to see if Mormons are polygamists, but now I'm jealous of the fact that Valentina is probably married to Ella (as well as Miss, but whatever. The point is, I'm not with the girl I love, and this creepy bitch is!).

"Are you sure about that?"

"That Valentina is his wife? Definitely."

"How…?" I start, but I'm not sure how to continue. I don't really get why this girl seems to know so much about vampires and… *ping!*

"Mormons only have one wife!" I say triumphantly, as Google provides.

"It's not important," insists Chibi. "What's important is that Miss is a vampire and if he hasn't already, soon he'll have two brides!"

"So, what do you want me to do about it?" I ask caustically. I'm surprised she has an answer for a question that was honestly rhetorical.

"Well, if you want to be with Ella, you could always kill Valentina," Chibi says. She sounds perfectly reasonable as though she's just come up with an alternative to a broken lightbulb.

Kill a vampire? Absolutely mental.

"I'd get arrested," I whine.

"Would you? There'd be no body," Chibi challenges me and I look at her, surprised.

"Seriously?"

"It just sort of bursts into dust and blows away."

"Okay, how the actual do you know that?" I ask. She looks at me, almost with a moment of sadness.

"You don't remember me from school, do you?" she replies, and I want to say yes so desperately, but we're at the point of the conversation where I realise that she will absolutely know if I'm lying or not. So, I don't bother. "Because I'm the nerd that everyone didn't want to know. The weird one sitting by themselves in the playground, because no one wants to talk to the crazy chick who believes in vampires and whose father disappeared because he was totally taken by a vampire, despite the fact that no one believes it."

Oh.

This all rings a bell, and I'm definitely starting to remember a girl that was too weird to be friends with. Oh, God, was I the one who told Ella they shouldn't be friends? I sort of remember having that conversation. Oh, wow, this is awful. I don't say anything, but I feel like absolute shit.

"It's fine," Chibi says, her eyes lowered, but I think she saw something in mine.

"So, you think I should kill Valentina?"

"Take her place, and you'll be with Ella forever," Chibi replies.

That's... not as insane as it sounds.

When Ella finally joins us, I ask her to describe Miss' house.

"Uhmm... I don't know," Ella says.

"Have you never been inside his house?" I ask, and it's razor sharp.

"He lives with his granddad, and his granddad doesn't like visitors."

"Sounds like an excuse." Actually, I stand by that, because... what?

"Look," Ella says, a little exasperated, "I think I have a photo maybe. I don't even understand why you're so curious about his house."

I suppose I'm glad that she doesn't press too hard on this particular point. But here's the thing, the more I thought about Chibi's idea, the more it sort of appeals to me. Like, I know I'm full on obsessed with Ella, but I am truly in love with her, and the thought of being with her forever is something I'm totally on board with. I mean, okay, so there's the fact we'd be married to Miss, who is apparently a vampire, and I'm not entirely certain what that means in practical terms. But I pretty much won't grow old and hopefully there's some way around having to kill people.

Chibi's research is extensive, and all in her head, which I would argue is a little weird. She says that vampires can actually go out during the day, but they do get burnt, so they will do their thing during the night and probably will be asleep during the day because they still need sleep. This definitely applies to Miss and Valentina (and also Ella, but in truth her lifestyle hasn't changed much since becoming a vampire. She just lost her amazing tan, which saddens me, but you know).

"I don't get why Ella isn't living with the other two," I say when Chibi tells me what she thought the living arrangements would be.

"Oh, it's probably a case of transitioning," Chibi replies with easy blasé.

"What?"

"Well, you know," annoyingly, Chibi shrugs. "Like, if Ella just moved in permanently with Miss, her mum might lose her shit or whatever." It's a fair point. I know Ella's mum, and she would be furious with Ella having married without telling her, let alone move in with a guy she barely knew and having become a vampire.

Scratch that, I don't really know how she'd react to the vampire bit. I don't think it would be well though.

"So how do I get to this Valentina?" I ask, and Chibi sits back in the chair, her white-blonde hair turned blue by the lights of the bar.

"You need to sneak in during the day, find Valentina's bedroom and…" Chibi mimes staking someone, almost falling off the chair with enthusiasm. The guy getting drinks behind the bar is someone I also think I went to school with, but he's drunk and just laughs at Chibi looking like a knob. Hopefully he didn't hear our plan to commit murder.

Oh, wait.

"But it's murder, right?" I ask and for the first time, I do feel pretty awful about it.

"Not really," Chibi reasons. "She's dead. Vampires are undead. So.. dead."

"But," I argue, "she's sentient. She's got a brain, she can think and feel and all the rest of it, can't she? She won't want to die. I mean properly die."

"Well, maybe not," Chibi agrees. "I guess it's up to you, about what you want to do. Either do the deed or… lose Ella forever."

Poo.

Skip forward to me trying to convince Ella to tell me what the layout of Miss' house is so I can go in and murder the woman that might be her wife. That last bit does incense me; I'm slightly more determined to go through with it. Ella gives me her phone and I look at the pictures.

"Seriously, he lives here?" I say, and Ella shrugs. All I'm thinking is that if I'm going to be a vampire bride, there's no way we aren't decorating this hole.

"I might move in with him one day," Ella says, as if I don't already know that is actually her plan. "But it might need some sprucing up." Excellent. We're on the same page. Although…

"Wish I could move in with you," I say, measuring the despondency in my voice.

"Oh," Ella says, and my heart rises that she sounds sad. "Oh," and this time there's the hint of an idea in her voice. "Maybe you can, one day." And she gives me that look, as her tongue touches the side of her mouth.

Well. We're good to go.

The door to the house is open, and I'm strolling in without a care in the world, a mallet and a broom handle that I broke. It's also a bit of a pit. Like, the house is just darkened rooms, with shades pulled down so the light can't get in. Definitely unpleasant. Like, definitely.

There's also a weird smell, like… like, maybe blood, but dried blood. I can't exactly explain it, but it just all feels off. I don't like it.

There are a lot of rooms for me to look in, but most of them are empty. I find the master bedroom and Miss is clearly asleep on the bed. Ella is on a couch, also asleep, looking gorgeous even though her hair is tousled and she's drooling.

Then there's Valentina. She's on another couch. She's very beautiful, and innocently serene. I really haven't thought this through.

This is so awkward.

I place the broomstick just above her chest and slam the mallet down. I'm actually terrified that it works. She awakes and looks at me with utter incomprehension.

"Why?" she murmurs, and then, just as Chibi said, she starts to lose colour, and crumbles.

I turn, pretty shaken by what has happened, and standing before me are Miss and Ella.

"What have you done?" Ella asks, and Miss has nothing but unchecked fury in his eyes.

Here goes nothing.

"I can't live without you Ell. I'll do whatever it takes to be with you forever. Please, Miss, just give me this." I lower my head, trying to bow.

"You're surrendering to me?" Miss asks, surprised, and I nod. He looks at me curiously.

And then he's on me.

I wake up, and I'm lying with Ella draped across me, but holding me in a fashion. I can't lie, it's pretty much everything I've wanted for years, and it's amazing. I mean, sure, I've got pain in my neck, but it's throbbing less, and I do feel a weird hunger. Also, yeah, the light from the window is a little harsher than it used to be.

On the plus side, turns out Miss isn't all that interested in his brides. He likes the hunt, apparently, and he likes to be the boss, but now that he has Ella and me, he's happy to let us do our thing while he does his. There was mention of us having to find his victims or something, but I glossed over that. It'll probably come back to bite me in the ass at some point, but truthfully, if I'm forced to go hunting for him, there're a few bullies who are gonna regret calling me 'pipe cleaner'.

As I get up, more comes back to me from last night. I remember Ella saying something about how Miss' true goal is to get affection from the other bride, who apparently doesn't have much time for him.

Another bride? Awkward.

When the doorbell rings, Ella grumbles in her sleep and I don't hear Miss stirring, so I go to the door. Who's there?

Chibi.

"Hey," she says with a big grin, and pushes past me to enter. "So, all worked out well, then? Tina's desecrated?"

"Tina?"

"Valentina. I just call her Tina. I am not a fan," Chibi says. The cogs in my brain are starting to tick over.

"Wait," I say. Chibi looks at me, the grin not disappearing. "You're the third bride?"

"I guess so," she says, and as she licks her lips, I see the teeth, which makes me unconsciously run my tongue along my own teeth. The points are there.

"The one Miss is desperate for?"

"'Fraid so."

"The one who isn't desperate for him?" I feel like I'm recapping a K-drama for a friend.

"Even more 'fraid so," Chibi smiles apologetically. "But there's someone I've been obsessed with for a while, and you know what it's like when your heart locks in on someone."

Too true.

"Why don't you make a move on him? Or her?" I ask, a little confused.

"Oh," Chibi says innocently, "I did." And with that she kisses me, with as much passion as I kissed Ella last night. When it's over she says, "I think it worked out okay, right?"

And with a little giggle, she heads off into the house.

Oh, indeed.

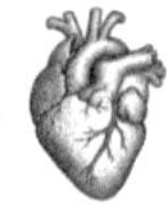

Come Back to Me

R A Purtill

The day I opened the door to the two gentlemen who were there to see my master, I should have been suspicious. When the large one tripped on the rug and shivered, nearly dropping the box he carried, I should have thought more of it. It was a warning. The presence of these two should have alerted me to the nature of my master's recent project, but such an arrival was the first of its kind, and it was not my place to question the master's guests. I led them through to the parlour to wait and went to prepare refreshments. When I returned with tea and the poppy-seed cake left over from the mistress' wake, my master was with them. They were in deep conversation so they did not notice me as I placed the tray on the low table. I'm used to feeling unseen. Even when the mistress was alive and even though she was friendly to me, I moved about the manor and no one noticed me.

Until that day the master did.

After the gentlemen departed, the master called for me to follow him to a wing of the manor where I had never been allowed. I couldn't imagine what he could want. My duties were to care for my mistress and when she died the master let me stay to keep house, but his laboratory was out of bounds. The room was like a wonderland. Lining the shelves were all manner of glass containers holding specimens. Others were filled with bright coloured liquids bubbling above a burner. The master led me to a long table and the sharp smell of disinfectant burnt my eyes. Something was covered by a sheet which he pulled off with a flourish. I gagged into my handkerchief.

"Mistress!"

She was all laid out, pale and exposed.

"I need your help to bring her back to me." His tone was casual, as if this were a mundane, routine task.

Before I could respond, he took up a shiny instrument and with precise movements, he sliced into the body. The sound of squelching flesh was followed by a line of blood across the torso. I had expected it to run like red fingers down to the table, where it might gather in little pools, but it did not. Then the crack of bone echoed like thunder as he pulled at the ribcage. His face shone with anticipation.

"Now she will come back to me."

He withdrew the contents of the box our recent visitors had brought and presented it to me. "A new heart is all she needs," he said.

One of my duties was to clean the library but the task took me longer than required as I always found the master's books so fascinating. From them I learnt what a heart looked like, and this was no heart of flesh. He placed it into my mistress' body, even so, and it sat in the chest cavity like a stone.

"And I gave good coin for it too," he said, releasing it and tossing it aside.

Two days later my master's sister arrived. As she entered the foyer, a vase of flowers fell from the sideboard. She scolded my master for his clumsiness, but I know he was nowhere near to make it fall. Later, as I cleaned it up, I remember a chill breeze blew the nearby curtains and I told myself it must have been that which caused the accident.

Miss Helen's plan was for an extended stay to comfort her grieving brother, but my master had something else in mind. Three days later a scream alerted me, and I ran to the laboratory. Miss Helen lay still and silent in her blood-soaked dress.

At the table my master held a mouldy lump which oozed through his fingers.

"This gangrenous mass will not bring her back to me."

It was then I understood what my mistress had told me about her sister-in-law: "A jealous, cantankerous woman for whom nothing was good enough" and yet, as my mistress explained, she was jealous of her brother. This green heart was proof.

"That is not the heart for you, sir," I said.

And that was when my master noticed me.

"A pure innocent heart like yours is what we need," he said.

He regarded me for such a long time, and with such a look of expectation in his bright eyes, I became uneasy. When his gaze went from me to the body on the table, I fully understood his intentions. What was I to do? The Manor was all I had, my position there my only opportunity.

I hid in my locked quarters, overwhelmed by the sound of my fearful heart, but thankful it was still in place. When he knocked on my door later, I refused to answer, but as his footsteps retreated, I peeked out to see him holding that gruesome instrument. No longer shiny but stained by his obsession. I gripped my chest to reassure myself my heart was still there. Mine was never the heart to bring Mistress Suzanna back.

That evening the disturbance in my room caused me to wake with a jump. A shimmering presence floated at the end of my bed.

"Leave this place." The familiar voice reverberated through me.

"Mistress Suzanna?"

When I remained paralysed, the apparition swung around the room throwing clothes from my cupboard to my carpet bag.

"Save yourself."

Fear quickened me, and I ran to call the master.

When I arrived at the laboratory, my master and the ghost of my mistress were locked in a bizarre standoff. He stood pale and paralysed beside the table and she hovered above her corpse.

"Harold, you must stop this."

"No, you must come back."

She swooped around his head until he spun and staggered against the table. He gripped the edge, and her glowing apparition moved in close. An understanding passed between them and in that moment realisation dawned on my master's face. He bowed his head.

"Only my heart can bring you back." He turned to me with the most horrible request. "You must put my heart in her body."

"But Master... "

"Do not deny me, Mary." He had never used my name before.

Mistress Suzanna's ghost swayed and sighed, anticipating her return to the living. Both my master and my mistress now pleaded with me. She to live, he to die for the one he loved. And there was I stranded between life and death with a power and responsibility no housemaid should ever have.

My master handed me the knife and when he saw

my hesitation, he enclosed his hand over mine and pushed the blade into himself. His last act was to remove his heart and with only the power of love to animate him, he placed it in the open chest of my mistress. The apparition faded altogether and in the same gasp with which my master died, the mistress returned to life.

"Now do as I say, Mary." Those words always preceded some instruction she had for me, as she did now. She directed me in the stitching of her chest and the removal of the master's body.

Mistress Suzanna came into an inheritance from the master, and we now live quietly, away from the city. When visitors come to the door, my mistress tells them the master died of a broken heart.

Wings in the Shadows

Fiona Emily

HIM

He sat on the corner edge of the building, legs dangling in the breeze, and watched. The drone of city noise echoed in the streets below. Above, stars flickered in the distance, their brightness held back by heavy clouds. All was quiet.

The air was crisp, but tinged with the bitter tang of smog.

He glanced below, like he had too many times already, distracted from the horizon he was supposed to be patrolling, that wired sensation deep within his chest.

Finally, stories below, the door opened. He held his breath, unable to still the thrill of anticipation buzzing through him.

A figure stepped into the night.

Her.

Flame red hair cascaded down her back. He breathed in the sight of her, feeling the knot ease within his chest. The soft curls of her hair, nestled against the crisp white shirt she wore after her late evening shift. Lanky heels threaded between long fingers, practical joggers on her feet that she always wore for her walk home.

She remained there, paused by the closed door, as if she didn't want to move. There was something off about her tonight. A lilt to her shoulders. Hesitation in her steps. As he observed more closely, he saw her swipe at her face.

Tears. She was wiping away tears.

He reacted without thought, flinging himself off the building, wings furling out against the rush of wind.

Who could have done this? Who could have made her cry?

It wasn't until he was partway down, air surging past, that he thought about what he was doing.

Did he intend to land in front of the girl and demand to know who hurt her? She had no clue who he was. What did he think that would achieve, other than giving her a heart attack? It was likely she had no inkling of the threats that existed around her, the watchers that moved above to protect those below.

No, he needed a different plan, something less foolish, less direct.

His wings rustled as they tilted, sending him careening off his planned course. He landed silently on the cobbled footpath, arching his back to fold in his wings, tucked safely beneath his black tunic, out of sight.

A misty rain started to fall.

It took all of a few swift strides to reach her trembling form, still standing in front of the door.

"Miss?" he asked, voice quiet. "Are you quite alright?" With a bow, he presented a folded tissue in his palm.

She looked up at him, eyes wide.

His throat closed in on itself. He had memorised her face. At least he'd thought so, in those quiet distant moments when he watched her. But this close, the curve of her pink lips, the depth of those glistening green eyes, the copper curls, how they bobbed as she lifted her head, one in particular covering the raised scar along her cheekbone, was a sight to behold.

"You," she stammered, staring up at him, face quirked in surprise. "They said you were watching. That you would come..."

They? His breath seized.

He couldn't be that predictable, could he? And yet, as he sorted through the memories of the woman he loved so many years before, there was an uncanny resemblance to her. The red hair may have been the first thing that drew him, but it was the multiple small moments he'd witnessed since; the kind words to those she served in the bar, how diligently she cared for the old man in the unit next door, how she tended to the plants on the sill of her tiny flat. The simplest of things that had him yearning to know her. As though his heart already did.

She gripped his hand. "You need to go."

It was hard to focus on words with her fingers set upon his skin, evoking an electric response. How long had it been since he'd felt anything? But this? Now? With her?

"Listen to me. You need to GO." Her palm pressed against his chest, but it lacked conviction, as though she herself couldn't bear the thought of them parting.

"They've planned an attack. They know about her, the one you loved. They expected you to come for me. They're waiting just around the next corner." A tear leaked from one of her green eyes.

He couldn't grasp the depth of her urgency, not as he watched that tear skim down her cheek. A knuckle intercepted its path. It wasn't enough, he couldn't help himself from stretching his fingers out, marvelling at the softness of her skin. She closed her eyes as if memorising his touch. As if he wasn't alone in this pivotal moment.

Her hand closed over his. Warm. Gentle. "They plan to trap you."

"You needn't fear for me. I am…"

"I know what you are. As do they." Her green eyes flashed with emotion. "Please." Her body trembled. "They want to rid the city of watchers."

The earnestness with which she spoke sent his heart thundering. She was trying to protect him, when all he wanted was to protect her. "Let me get us out of here."

"I can't." She pulled away.

The loss of her hand from his felt like he'd been wrenched in two. Left teetering in the rustle of wind, lost and more alone than ever.

"I can protect you." His words were a vow, a promise, for he knew it to be true. Watcher or no, forbidden or not, he would protect her with his everything.

"I don't need your protection." Defiance flashed in her gaze.

"But I need yours?" He couldn't help the smile that lifted his lips, this woman so much more than he'd anticipated. No clue of who or what he was.

She glared at him. It only made him smile more.

Perhaps the trap had already been set.

What awaited around the corner seemed of little consequence.

It was already too late, ensnared as he was.

For her.

HER

Bile surged up her throat. No matter how much she tried to breathe, she felt the burn and fully expected any moment it would spill out of her. Body stiff, she stood there, door closed behind her, staring at the wet cobbled footpath, trying to cope with the new reality she'd found herself in.

Tears burned her eyes.

What she wouldn't give to go back. Twenty minutes was all. She would have gone home as usual, early, never to be privy to the horrors that existed beyond her simple problems. Fear curled in her gut. She wasn't sure if she'd ever get that image out of her mind. The smell was bad enough, without looking at that horrible fanged mouth. A shiver ran down her spine. He was a hulking mass of threaded muscle and bone. Gangly, distorted. Dangerous. Predatory. She'd have nightmares, she was sure of it. But that was something to worry about later.

Lead the watcher into the ambush and you will be safe.

She closed her eyes against the surge of panic that wanted to consume her. That was his command. What she had to do. Just walk down the street. Pretend everything was normal, that her life wasn't under threat. Get whoever this watcher was to follow. Simple enough.

Misty rain fell from the heavens, the night, dark as sin. But it didn't register. Not after what she knew.

She had to do it; there was little other choice. Their war had nothing to do with her; she'd had no clue of their existence until moments ago. She would walk around that corner up ahead, making sure he followed, to save her life.

Shoulders heaved upright, looking straight ahead, she determinedly took a step.

"Miss? Are you quite alright?"

The voice came out of nowhere. As if of the

shadows, a hand with a tissue held out for her.

Body tense, she took in the figure before her. Dark clothing barely held his lithe powerful frame. Icy pale eyes tracked her every moment. It was hard to look beyond that swirling blue, turbulent as though infinity existed within.

"You," she stammered, feeling completely unhinged, like the world had been redefined in one brief moment. His otherness obvious, despite his attempts otherwise. "You're one of them." The one they wanted. From above. "They said you were watching, that you would come…"

She squeezed her lips shut, realising all too late what she'd said. Any attempt of pretending was gone. There were so many other things she could have said, should have said, and yet in that moment… her brain seemed to short circuit. Now he knew she knew what he was…

What was she going to do?

She peeked up at him. His gaze trailed across her skin, as if committing her to memory. It was hard not to do the same. He was beautiful. Beguiling. Strong jaw, thick brows, dark curls tied at the nape of his neck. But beauty could be deceiving.

Except he held a tissue. A tissue.

A white flag of sorts, proof he saw her distress, which suggested he'd been watching. Or stalking her?

A lump formed in her throat. She'd been told she had the same red hair as his love. That's why he was here. That was the extent of it. And yet… when he looked at her, it felt intimate, like it meant… more.

She shook her head. Damned hair, why couldn't she have been a brunette? And what was she supposed to do now? Walk on? Hope he followed? Would he follow?

Squaring her shoulders, she reminded herself of what was important. She was in danger, she needed to save herself.

She turned away from him, planning to walk towards the mouth of the alley without another word.

Except she couldn't. Something held her in place. The wrongness of her intentions, vibrating on some deeper level.

She reached for his hand, before she even realised what she was doing. "You have to go."

He just stared at her, glancing between her face and where their hands met.

Hadn't he heard her? "Listen to me. You need to GO." Her hand shifted to push him away, but she couldn't summon the ability to follow through.

Tears scorched her eyes. She knew what this meant. What she risked. Her chest burnt at the rightness, or the wrongness, she couldn't be sure, but the words were already on her lips. "They've planned an attack. They know about her, the one you loved. They expected you to come for me. They're waiting just around the next corner."

She thought he would sink back into the darkness, not place his hand against her cheek, not swipe away her tear. His touch was like the sun itself, leaving a scorching trail. She didn't even realise her hand rose to cup his, until their skin melded together. Oh, how she wanted to sink against his promise of warmth, which was confusing in itself. How could she feel this way? Did it matter with what they faced?

"They plan to trap you."

"You needn't fear for me," his voice rumbled. "I am…"

"I know what you are. As do they." Sorrow pierced her, a tremor filling her limbs. "Please. They want to rid the city of watchers."

"Let me get us out of here." His words were a whisper, and she closed her eyes against the brief second of possibility, pushing it away before it could grow into something.

"I can't." She let her hand fall. Took a step back. They would just find her again.

"I can protect you."

Her back stiffened. She wasn't someone who needed saving, as pathetic as she may seem. "I don't need your protection." This was her problem to fix. Whatever happened, she had no choice but to walk around that corner. If he didn't follow, maybe they would think her unimportant enough to leave her alone.

"But I need yours?" The arrogant smile that graced his lips could have lit up the night sky, it was so luminous.

She glared at him, then forced herself to look away. Take a step from him and ignore the traitorous reaction of her heart.

The corner of the building loomed ahead. Her

heart pounded so loud it drowned out every other sound. She had no clue if he was following, just that she needed to keep going. To do what needed to be done.

Body tensed, her heels held firmly against her chest—a weapon ready to strike, she stepped around the corner.

Breath whooshed from her chest. No one waited in the shadows. It was empty.

Relief poured through her. For all of two seconds.

Dark masses dropped from above. Four, then five. A crack of lightening sliced through the night, revealing the horror that surrounded her. Yellow eyes. Dripping saliva. Fangs. Hides the size of an elephant.

Oh, how naïve she'd been.

And stupid.

It wasn't a trap just for the watcher, but her too. These creatures weren't going to let her live, not with the way they looked at her. Hungered for her.

She did need his protection.

Warm fingers touched the nape of her neck. A reassurance. A presence at her back.

Dark wings billowed out as he surged forward, letting out a guttural growl that pierced the night air. He was a sight to behold, a murderous force of nature that stood poised to defend her.

The way her heart reacted to the sight, she knew was in trouble. Not from the danger they faced. But from the winged force that made the earth tremble.

Her watcher.

Chatsworth House

A J R Fraser

Stretched out on the king-sized bed, his eyes closed as she gently caressed his face, David's imagination fuelled his desires. Her fingertips whispered across his cheek as she passionately nibbled and sucked his neck. His heart raced and his breath tightened, hands tensing under crumpled white sheets. It was only a quick holiday stay at Chatsworth House, but the dream of waking to this every morning brought a smile to his face.

"I wish this could be forever," David sighed.

Her delicate fingers danced over his chest, circled his nipples, and then outlined his abs, before they descended under the sheets.

Suddenly, the door creaked. "Babe, are you up yet?" Abbie called from across the room. "I got you a coffee."

David's eyes shot open and he sat bolt upright. His girlfriend had just entered the room, but who was in bed with him? His head swivelled franticly. Nothing. A tiny shriek escaped his lips as he pulled the top sheet tight to his chest.

"You good, babe?" Abbie placed his cup on the bedside table, then returned to her side. "This place is like, nice. I can't wait to post on my Instagram. Like, I thought the kitchen in this crusty old castle would be gross. But like, no." She stopped, sipped then continued. "We'll have to get going soon. I've booked a personal tour on the moors in like, thirty minutes and with the heavy fog it's going to be like, amazing. I've got chills." While seated on the edge of the bed Abbie's phone pinged and she quickly picked it up. "Oh Em Gee, my recent pics are like, really popular."

He rubbed the back of his neck as goosebumps crawled up his spine. Who? What? His mind raced as he glared at his girlfriend's lips - silently dancing. He held onto the sheet as his head slowly rotated to inspect the room a second, then third time. Nothing.

Abbie stood, retrieved David's clothes from the cupboard and tossed them onto the bed. Her lips continued to dance as she paraded around the room. Stop. Sip. Check phone. Mumble. "Hey, are you listening to me? Hurry up couch-boy, I'm not your mum, you're twenty-four. Get dressed, we haven't got all day." Abbie leant down and held his chin. "You're such a dope." She then moved in for a kiss but reeled back in disgust. "What's that on your neck? Like, is it a rash? Did something bite you? Are you sick?"

David swallowed as he covered his throat. "I... Ah... Um..." Words failed him. "I thought..." He looked towards the door. "No... You were just here." David tapped the bed beside him. "And then you came in... With coffee. Where were you?"

"I just told you." Abbie shrugged as she gathered up her oversized handbag and her cell phone. "I went down to reception and got us a coffee from the kitchen. My followers are going to love my next posts... The fog, the moors, Oh, I'm like, so excited. Now hurry up, Travis is waiting for us."

"Go not upon the moors," a gentle female voice whispered into his ear.

David sprang out of the bed. "Who said that?"

"What? Travis, he's my private tour guide." She gathered her lip gloss and began applying it while she continued to talk. "He says, I'm going to be like following in the footsteps of Sherlock Holmes or Maid Marion and you can like, film it. He's even got me a costume. Like, amazing."

"I beseech thee, David, venture not upon the moors." That beautiful, strange voice in an old English accent whispered again.

"Who. Who said that?"

"Travis did," Abbie snapped back, as she adjusted her dress, applied and reapplied another layer of makeup while glaring into the full-length mirror.

"What's wrong with you, David? Haven't you been listening to anything I've been saying? Like, um, I'm doing a tour of Chatsworth House and the moors and its…"

"Abbie did you hear that other voice?" David's head turned from side to side.

"Venture not upon the moors," the soft female voice reiterated.

"There it is again." David snatched up his clothes and quickly dressed.

"Like, what is wrong with you?" Abbie rolled her eyes. "I don't like this, David. You're really bringing down the vibe. Um… my friends said that you'd be like, bad for my socials."

"Someone's saying we shouldn't go out on the moors," David repeated.

"David, get a grip. Like, I haven't got time for this." Abbie let out a dramatic sigh, then tightly clutched her designer bag to her chest and stomped towards the door. "If you don't want to go, just say so. I'll get Travis to like, take my pics instead."

"Something feels funny, I don't think—"

Abbie snorted with a pinched nose. "You don't think. Well, then." She then quickly stepped through the doorway, slammed it behind her and screamed to emphasize her dramatic exit.

Grabbing his shoes, David dashed towards the door. Chasing after her like he always did.

"Venture not." A soft lullaby voice sighed. "I beseech thee."

He reached for the door handle, then from the

corner of his eye he caught a glimpse of something in the mirror. A beautiful young woman, naked, on the end of his bed. Long, dark, wavy hair cascading past her shoulders, covering her voluptuous curves. In haste David twisted around, tripped, bounced off the dresser and then face-planted onto the floor.

"Are thee well?" The mysterious girl knelt and placed a reassuring hand on his shoulder. "I meant thee no fright."

He groaned as he rolled over and looked up into her beautiful emerald eyes. "Who? Who? Who?"

"Art thou an owl?" she giggled. A beautiful girl in her early twenties, stood up and stepped back. Her long white lace gown billowed around her like a morning mist. "Forgive me, if thou ist in pain," she said with a smile.

"Who are you?"

"I am Lady Mary Cavendish, the firstborn daughter of Sir William Cavendish, the second Duke of Devonshire."

"Where did you come from?" David slowly stood while rubbing his bruised cheek.

Mary's grin broadened. "Behold Chatsworth House, mine home." She gestured to everything around her. "'Tis mine own room." As Mary sat on the end of the bed, her clothes vanished in a swirl of mist.

"Woooooow." David jumped backwards, tripped on his discarded shoes, smacked the back of his head on the dresser and passed out.

"David… David…" Mary knelt over his prone body as the mist floated around her curves and restored the gorgeous white lace gown. She smoothed back his short light brown hair. "David... Canst thou hear mine voice? I beseech thee, please wake up." She pressed a hand to his chest and felt his heartbeat. Thump. Thump. Thump. The grey t-shirt that he wore rose and fell with every breath, but he did not wake.

She gently stroked his cheek while humming an old sonnet for several minutes. "Oh, mine sleeping beauty." Holding her long dark locks away from her face, she leant forward and softly pressed her lips to his.

David responded, savouring the intimacy and returning the desire as his eyes blinked open. "Wait," he moaned, stopped, and then looked up into those stunning green eyes. A true longing in his heart that felt forever dormant, sparked emotions he'd never known. Was he to fear or embrace this new sensation? His heart rate increased.

"Are thee well?" Mary smiled.

"I feel a bit sore, a little strange, a little embarrassed, and a whole lot confused." He rubbed the back of his head. "Who? What? Where? Plus, what's with your clothes?" He reached out and gently caressed the lacy gown, unsure of its existence. Yes, it was real.

"Pray forgive me, for it is that accursed bed." Mary slowly stood and helped David to his feet. "The Bed of Desires," she added with a heavy heart.

A little wobbly on his feet, David staggered forward, but Mary's quick actions caught him before he fell.

"So, you're a ghost. You're not real." He scratched his head. "But how do you feel so real?"

David went to lie down on the bed, but instead Mary grabbed the back of his shirt and guided him over to the chair by the window.

"Well... nay, I'm not really a spectre. I am desire incarnate." She smiled. "Permit me to recollect." David slowly nodded. "My father, the Duke of Devonshire had betrothed me to the son of another noble house, as custom demands."

David watched as Mary paced, while vapours of mist trailed behind her.

"Yet my soul yearned for greater pursuits. I longed to voyage afar. To set sail for the Americas. Or, to lend aid unto our brave countrymen who did battle against the Jacobite uprising in Scotland. I had no desire for idle pursuits in parlours and conservatories, with prattling old ladies, and thus discuss frivolous tales they had read in books. Yap, Yap, Yap." Mary's hands and face overdramatised her words. "Nay, I yearned to live."

David frowned. "Okay, I'm getting some of that."

"I beheld mine own kin, siblings, cousins and family friends thus perish, cut down in their tender years, never they to seize their heart's longings. I did swear then and there, I shan't become some thrall, nor a wife kept in idle servitude. So, I am to flee." She paused and wiped tears from the corners of her eyes. "But alas, at two and twenty years, an evil witch's hex would befall me, and thus I and my hearts yearnings did wither and die unfulfilled and unremembered."

Mary walked slowly towards the king-sized bed. "And this, then, is my curse, the yoke I bear – to bring to pass not mine own wishes, but the desires of others."

David stood up and moved to the bed. "So, you're saying, the bed is cursed." He reached out and placed a hand on the white sheets. "But how do you know what I desire?"

"Thou dost desire intimacy." Mary put a hand to her chest, and drew in a long breath. "I can sense it and thus, I do desire it likewise." She nestled into David's arms and nuzzled his neck.

"But Abbie was in this bed too." David stepped back and held Mary's shoulders. "What did she desire?"

"She dost desire notoriety." Mary replied. "Or as ye sayeth... popularity."

David nodded. It was knowledge his head knew, but his heart did not want. The thought of being stuck in a relationship that had no future, no heart, and did not fulfil his wishes, felt like a cage. It would fester and poison their emotions, and eat them both from inside. Toxic.

He looked at Mary, this beautiful young girl forever trapped, forever cursed, and his heart sank. She'd never fulfil her own emotions or desires, and was only a slave to others. He knew that he could change his life, but what about hers?

"Is there any way we can break this curse?" David queried.

"I know not." Mary sat down on the bed and her clothes evaporated in a swirl of white mist. "Maybe, if we do not give in to our desires, the curse shall be lifted."

David eye's nervously darted from Mary's naked form, to the ceiling, back to Mary, then to the ceiling again. "I... I... I think we can... ahhh... do that."

A few hours later.

With cheeks flushed and a little out of breath, David quietly closed the door behind him, used his cellphone to send a quick text and then wandered down to reception. Ting, Ting, Ting. He tapped the bell on the counter and a short, bald man came out of the office to receive him.

"Welcome sir, how can I help you?"

"I, ah..." David scratched his head. "I was wondering... do you sell your beds?"

"Is everything alright, sir?"

"Um, yes. Why do you ask?"

The bald man grimaced. "Two reasons. One. People don't usually buy beds from hotels," he said while shaking his head. "And two, Sir, you don't seem to have any pants on."

The Moors

A J R Fraser

Abbigail stepped out of the elevator into the lobby to find Travis waiting by the main entrance. The tall, muscular man with short dark hair had a smile that would inspire a million subscribers. He looked mighty fine in denim jeans and a buttoned-up, long sleeve, light blue shirt.

She sauntered over to him, extended the selfie-stick with her cell phone attached, and hit record.

"Welcome fellow Nomads, I'm here in Devonshire U.K., at the lovely Chatsworth House." Her fake smile beamed. "And like, I'm about to do a tour of the amazing gardens, the medieval woods, the hedge maze, and the moors, with..." she swung the selfie-stick around to capture them both in frame, "the incredible Travis."

Travis smiled and gave a confident thumbs-up.

"Okay. Now you wanted the inclusive tour... right?" He presented her with a large trunk nearby full of old clothes. "So, I've got several period costumes. There's Sherlock Holmes, Dr. Watson, Mrs. Cavendish—the Lady of Chatsworth House, Robin Hood, Maid Marion and even the local Witch of Chatsworth Woods."

Abbie focused her phone on herself. "Okay, everyone, I've been given several options to create a character for this fully immersive tour. Um... like, let me know in the comments which one you think I should wear." She clicked her phone off and turned to her guide. "Travis, can you snap some photos of me in all the costumes?"

Behind the reception desk stood a short, bald man serving a tall and mysterious male with intense eyes. Baldy called out from across the lobby. "Hey Travis, did you hear about the girl that disappeared on the moors?"

Travis shook his head and then turned to Abbie. "Ignore him, he's just trying to scare you." He reached out for Abbie's cell phone, and then over the next several minutes snapped numerous photos while she posed provocatively in different costumes.

"Oh, slay!" Abbie screeched and then cackled whilst hidden under many layers of an old tattered, patchy grey dress. "Like, this is the one. I'm making this look fetch." To complete the outfit she donned an old, large wolf-head ring and then she applied an extra thick layer of dark eye shadow and mascara to complete the creepy appearance.

"Ah, the Witch of Chatsworth Woods. Scary," Travis commented.

The tour started with a 600-year historical walk through England's past. Royalty, Dukes, medieval myths, and mysterious deaths, but most of the information sailed over Abbigail's head. She was just happy capturing hundreds of images, standing beside ancient statues, manicured gardens and old Victorian architecture. Ding. Ding. Posted to Instagram.

On a few occasions Abbie thought she noticed the tall dark stranger from the reception following them as they wandered through the beautiful gardens and woods. She held up her selfie-stick and with a spooky voice, began her presentation. "Like, this fog is so creepy. It's like, giving me icky vibes. I can barely see my hand in front of me. So, let's travel back to when witches were real..."

Travis stepped into the frame. "In the early 1700s, it was documented that an evil witch had roamed these woods." He lowered his voice and feigned fear as his shifty eyes perused the area. "It was told she was hideous, covered in filth with black soulless eyes, and the air around her had the stench of death. The witch was reported to be in league with a mysterious beast that roamed the moors. And..."

"Wow... it's like, I've gone back three hundred years," Abbie whispered to the camera. The wolf-ring's eyes glowed red and in the distance they heard a hooting owl, 'Who... Who... Who...' The fog around them swirled thicker, the air smelt sweeter, and the forest closed in as the foliage condensed.

Nearby, a deep guttural growl echoed through the woods. "What was that?" Abbie swung the camera around. "Did you hear that?"

Travis put a finger to his lips. Shhhhhh. "You're going to be alright." A wicked grin spread on his face as he reached behind his back.

A twig snapped. A blur. Something rushed out of the fog. Travis was knocked off his feet. Abbie screamed and dashed farther into the woods. Holding up her selfie-stick she continued to yell between panicked gasps. "Something is after me! Ahhhh! Something is out there!"

The soup-thick fog swirled. Her heart raced as a wild howl trailed her. She looked around and found herself out on the moors. No path, dull light, limited visibility and alone. Abbie was lost. The panting of a feral animal neared and again her feet fled with haste, but after only several steps, she tripped. Fell. Then face planted into the dirty waters of a shallow pond. Covered in mud and slime, she crawled out of the pond and called out in panic.

"Help, Travis! Help me. Oh my God! Like, this is disgusting."

Abbie wiped her face and smeared dark makeup everywhere. Twisting around, she heard the approach of heavy footsteps. Thump. Scrape. Thump. Scrape. In a panic she searched for her phone, but couldn't find it anywhere.

"Abbie," Travis groaned as he slowly limped out of the fog. His shirt was shredded and covered in blood. "There's something big out there, and it got me. Are you okay?" He looked down at his mauled arm that hung limp by his side. The skin was peeled back and revealed muscles torn to the bone as blood dripped from his fingertips.

"I can't find my phone." Abbie reeled back from Travis and continued to look for it. Then she mumbled to herself, "Please help me. This is a dream. It can't be happening."

Travis limped closer as he drew a knife, "Abbie, I think it's over here. Come here, pretty girl, come to me." Concealing a hand behind his back, he beckoned her.

As she turned towards Travis, he raised the knife. But, off to the right, Abbie noticed a large, dark shadow as it rose in the mist, its muscular fur covered arm reached out and, in a flash, its deadly claws ripped across Travis's neck. He staggered, dropped the weapon, faced the heavens, screamed silently in pain and then fell to his knees. A shower of blood spurted from the deep gash across his throat as his eyes rolled back and he collapsed forward into the mud.

Covered in gore and mud, Abbie sobbed. "NO! No. No. Please. This must be a dream. What is happening?" She closed her eyes and continued to pray, then tried to scream, but no sound escaped. Muscles taut as her heart pounded so hard it felt like it was going to burst out of her chest. She wanted to run. Flee. But, her feet were frozen in fear.

HOOOOOWL! The creature's wail sent shivers down her spine. It stepped out of the fog, bent down, raked its hand along the open wounds of its prey and then proceeded to slowly lick its fingers. The large Were-Like-Thing crept closer, sniffing the air while licking its lips. A wild beast in denim jeans, with thick dark black fur—half wolf, half man. Slimy drool dripped from its blood-stained fangs.

Paralyzed with fear, Abbie whispered another prayer then swallowed dryly as the feral creature approached. Its strong aroma filled her nostrils, its pheromones powerful, sweet, magical, alluring, and arousing.

The beast slowly circled her, edging closer.

She reached out and put a gentle palm on its muscular chest and felt the deep reverberating rumble of every breath. The intense sensations of touch, scent, sight and sound overpowered her emotions. Fear evaporated.

There was an extraordinary feeling, a connection, like bonded spirits. Abbie felt everything within the beast. It was an emotional turmoil of rage, hate, love and yearning that battled for control. This intense attachment was akin to a merging of souls... It was something she'd never felt before, but fiercely craved. The creature's emotions were hers and her emotions were the beast's. They embraced and their heartbeats and breathing synced. Abbie snuggled into his long dark fur and felt more than warmth, more than comfort; it was a desire, a longing stronger than love. She couldn't contain herself as tears flowed, and the beast howled.

She reached up with a soothing hand and caressed the werewolf's neck and shoulders. Its hot breath tickled her neck. Calmness flowed within as she looked into its eyes. She'd never felt so alive, so attuned to another. She wanted nothing but to give everything, to continue these intense feelings. She inhaled more pheromones as her body tingled all over. Then the beast's ears pricked up and its head snapped around. Something was close. Abbie purred as the werewolf's heightened senses surged through her body.

A dark-haired girl in her early twenties wandered along the other side of the bog. The stranger stopped, startled, and with wild fear in her eyes, screamed then turned and fled into the thick fog. Her long flowing white gown whispered across the grassy moors.

Abbie felt a surge of adrenalin and let loose a guttural growl as she trailed the beast, also in pursuit of the young female. Her nostrils flared with the thrill of the chase.

The mysterious girl in white raced for home as the feral monster closed the distance. She hurried across the green fields of heather with her white lace gown gathered up in her hands. Her foot caught on something which sent her sprawling. She reached around for anything that might protect her and her hand landed on a metal rod with a shiny strange plate at the end. She swung the thing around wildly.

With a feral growl, the werewolf smashed the plate off the end of the metal stick and then lunged at the scared young girl.

Abbie flinched and grabbed her side, she hunched over and then fell to her knees as a terrible pain tore into her chest. Slowly, she regained her feet and staggered forward to find the werewolf, her soulmate, curled up on the ground, a metal rod protruding from its chest. Her selfie-stick. The creature released a painful moan as it struggled to breathe. It clawed at the dirt as he tried to stand but collapsed with a howl.

The strange girl stood up and raised her hands in defence. "Stand thee back, thou foul witch. Begone from hence!"

"What have you done?" Abbie screamed, as intense pain and wild emotions coursed through her body. Dropping to her knees beside the werewolf, she gently stroked the beast as it rasped and coughed up blood. Tears welled as Abbie turned to face the mysterious interloper. "Who are you?"

"Thou knowest not with whom thou speaketh. For I am Lady Mary Cavendish." Mary pronounced with her chin raised. "I am High-born, and thou is nothing but a hideous witch, in league with thy cursed beast. Begone, fiend! May Heaven's light cast thee back into das blackest pit whence thou crawled."

"Bitch." Abbie spat. "What..."

"Nay, Witch, it be thou."

"I curse you, for what you have done. I... curse...

you... Mary Cavendish." Abbie's high-pitched screech, layered with venom, echoed across the moors as the eyes of the wolf-head ring glowed red. "A curse that will rip from your soul all that you desire, everything. Your short, miserable life will go forever unfulfilled. For eternity you will be nothing but a slave to other's desires and perform stupid tricks only to please idiots. Like a common whore, your bed will be your burden. A bed of desires. You will feel nothing unless others are fulfilled."

"Nay." Fear flashed in Mary's eyes. "Be still thy foul mouth, witch."

Abbie tugged at the rags she wore, then raised her hands and hissed at Mary. "Like, you silly bitch, I'm an influencer. I'll destroy you on social media. I wish I could go back..."

The wolf-ring's eyes glowed and in the distance, a strange bell could be heard. Ting, Ting, Ting. The thick fog swirled as a wild gust picked up and a shaft of light reached through the clouds. Abbie felt strange as the mist lifted and the mysterious young girl named Mary faded away. It was just her and the beast in the open field.

The werewolf's body convulsed and thrashed on the ground, in a pool of blood it transformed into human form. The mysterious man groaned as he clutched at the selfie-stick that was still embedded in his chest.

"Easy... easy now." Abbie placed a calming hand on top of his and looked into those deep brown eyes. She could still see the wolf. "We need to get you help."

He looked up at Abbie. "Are you okay?"

"What?"

Cough. Cough. "Are you hurt? We should be safe, now."

She wiped away several specks of blood from his lips. "I'm okay, but what is going on?"

"Travis is..." He groaned, coughed, and closed his eyes. "Travis was a demon. I've been tracking him for several years." Cough. Cough. "He's taken girls... but, I finally got him. We got him."

Abbie wiped her hand across her confused face.

"This is... not real. A demon, a witch and a werewolf. Plus a strange girl that disappeared. Like, this is way too freaky. It's doing my head in."

She looked to her left and glimpsed her cell phone. Cracked and muddy. Abbie picked it up and wiped the screen. Ding. Ding. Ding. Her social media was on fire.

Ding. 'Love the Witch costume.'

Ding. 'I hope you're having a fun tour on the moors.'

Ding. 'Abbie I think we should take a break. We have different desires, and I wish you the best. David.'

The thrill she usually felt when receiving a like or comment was not there. It felt hollow. Empty. She looked down at the injured man beside her, into his soulful eyes and Abbigail knew the true feeling of a real connection.

Lost Time

Evelyn Caster

Callen stretched, weary muscles aching from the unfortunate position the dawn had caught him in as the sun slid down over the trees. He was rather surprised to find himself on the ground, after being halfway up a ladder before turning to stone.

His front door swung open, and Asaka sauntered out, holding a coffee out to him. As the warmth leached from the air, he drew it in from the cup. Definitely from the drink and not from the way she smiled, eyes crinkling in the corners, just for him.

"How did you end up like this?" she asked, gently blowing across the top of her own cup. Steam curled through the chill of the night air, brushing against his cheek like phantom fingers.

"Good question." He moved so they were shoulder to shoulder, and glanced out at the neighbourhood. The kids from the werewolf family across the road were tearing towards their house, yelling goodbye to their fae neighbour. Down the street, a trio of nattering witches bent together over a bush in Asaka's yard. As he watched, flowers bloomed, blood red, and the women cackled in delight.

Callen chanced a glance at Asaka, pale fingers wrapped around the blue mug, her skin glowing in the streetlight. As always, he wanted to pause and take her in. He turned back to his own mug before she caught him staring. Again.

She looked at him with a half-smile dancing on her lips. "Well?"

He took a drink and shrugged. "We met a shifter who made a town with a dragon."

Even when she rolled her eyes, it was elegant. "Not us. *You.* The book club was talking, you know."

"About me?" Callen snorted. He wouldn't put it past them. He was sure they should rename themselves the gossip club, but he didn't dare say it in front of their founder.

"The first gargoyles appeared in the 1220s. And by my calculation, that's how old you are."

He almost choked on a mouthful of liquid. "Are you calling me old?" It was a weak deflection, but it was better than saying nothing.

Hurt flashed across her face as Asaka pulled away.

"You don't have to tell me. It's not like we've known each other for centuries."

Tipping his head back, Callen's gaze fell on the first evening star, letting the rest of the world fade away. "It's not something I enjoy remembering."

Silence for a beat. "I'm sorry," Asaka's voice was smaller than he ever remembered hearing it. The clunk of her cup as she set it on the porch post had him sucking in a breath. Her heels clacked against the path as she made her way towards the gate.

"It happened at dawn," he said, voice barely a whisper.

Asaka paused. Her hearing good enough that he didn't have to say it any louder. He wasn't sure he could.

"My parents were both shifters, but the townsfolk thought Ma was a witch. She worked with herbs and healing. Had been teaching me some. Then, early one morning, a woman came through when they were out. Said she had a bit of a problem with her hair. Asked for my help." He was vaguely aware of Asaka drifting back towards him, but Callen knew that if he looked at her, he would never get the story out. "I turned around to tell my brother to get back inside, and when I turned back, she'd removed her headscarf, and I was looking at a nest of snakes."

"A gorgon?" Asaka whispered, briefly laying a cool hand on his arm. Tingles shot through the offending limb and fluttered around the heart he wasn't so sure was rock anymore.

Callen nodded. "My feet turned first, and the shock

forced my first change right as the sun rose. It's what saved me. Although we wouldn't realise it until that night, when the stone fell off, and I became human again."

"You were *the* first?"

A nod. "I'd hoped to be the last. But battle doesn't always work that way. I got stabbed or sliced or shot, and if my blood gets on the skin of another shifter, they turn the way I do." He took another drink, wishing it were whiskey instead of coffee. Hoping it would remove the boulder that lodged in his throat whenever he thought about that first day. "Can't say they're all mine though, because they can't do the same thing. Each generation is weaker. I can still slough off the stone if I need to during daylight, but the others aren't as fortunate."

"You can move in the day?" Asaka's eyes widened.

He knew if she had a heartbeat, it would have sped up. It had been a long, long time since she'd seen the sun, and everyone always wants what they can't have. He gave her another glance.

"It costs me." Callen picked up her cup from the porch and turned to go inside, trusting she would follow. "Why ask now?"

"We've known each other for so long, how have you never told me this before?" Callen could detect the genuine hurt underneath the practiced pout.

He wanted to snarl, to torment her the way those memories had once burnt him. Instead, he took a breath. It had been a long time since he'd snapped out of anger. "Same way I won't ever ask how you were turned."

Asaka flinched. "Thank you for telling me, despite how painful it was to share."

"Guess you'll have to cheer me up then." Callen forced a smile. "What's the book for this week?"

She blinked, her thick lashes fluttering.

Biting back a chuckle, Callen slowly counted, and reached seventeen.

"What happens if you're not a shifter?" she blurted. For a creature almost as old as he was, Asaka loathed awkward silences. Said they reminded her too much of 'coffin time.'

"That's the book?"

Running her tongue over the tip of a fang, she looked at him expectantly.

"Two things. They either die because I refuse to spill unnecessary blood, or—" Callen paused and tugged against his suddenly tight collar. He'd been about to mention that certain variants of supernaturals had a very different reaction to his blood.

"So death, or the little death?"

He scoffed. "You've been spending too much time around that French git."

"Not by choice," she muttered.

"What do you mean?" he growled.

Crossing the room towards him with swinging hips, Asaka ran a hand up his shirt buttons. "What happens to your clothing when you change?" As much as he may wish her touch was seductive, she was clinical, eyes clear and calculating.

She may not have aimed at being a temptress, but one part of his anatomy had not got the memo. *Friend. She is a friend.* "My theory is the excess fabric gets pushed into the wings."

Catching his gaze, Asaka leaned in , and he felt a puff of air leave her lungs and brush across his lips.

"My turn." He grasped her hips and turned to lift her onto the counter. It had been a habit of decades that Callen claimed was so he didn't have to stoop so much. Asaka wasn't much shorter than him, but she let him get away with the thin excuse. Almost as if she wanted his hands on her. He would never presume, even if she did automatically widen her legs so he could step between them. "Why do you get so close to me?"

Clarity dropped, and panic took its place. "What do you mean?" she asked before the calm mask slid back into place.

He drew closer, placing a finger under her chin and forcing her to look at him. "Everyone else thinks you're flirting when you do this with me. I've seen you do it with others, but you never get as close for as long as you do with me."

"Maybe they're not as obtuse," she blurted, then slapped a hand across her mouth, eyes wide.

"Asaka," he warned.

She shuddered, eyes rolling slightly.

"What was that?" he demanded. If he moved any closer, their chests would brush, and she'd be able to detect something straining at his zip that he'd rather she not know about.

"When you say my name…" she trailed off. "They said I should tell you."

"Tell me what?"

"Stop growling at me," Asaka pushed against him with no actual strength.

There were a few supernaturals who could take him in a fight, and they were both well aware that she was one of them.

"Are you flirting with me?"

"Would you be upset if I said yes?" she fluttered her eyelashes in a ridiculously overt manner.

But he knew her. Knew that she liked tea as black as her soul when she first work up. That she pretended to crave caramel, but preferred blood orange even though she hated how cliché it made her. Whenever one of them was away, they would always seek each other out when they returned. More than anything, he knew the next word out of his mouth had the ability to destroy four hundred years of friendship.

His gravelly voice rolled through the room. "No."

Asaka paused. "Does this mean I can finally kiss you?"

"Yes." Callen didn't even have to think.

Cautiously, she stretched, brushing her lips ever so gently over to his.

Sparks flared behind his eyes.

She gave a soft, barely there gasp.

"Did you feel that too?" he asked.

Grabbing fistfuls of his shirt, Asaka drew him in, devouring his mouth with her own. Callen crushed her against his chest, crouching so the counter shielded the overactive beast in his pants.

Hours, or maybe days later, the kissing slowed, and they rested their foreheads together, breathing heavily.

"Should have done that decades ago," Asaka said.

Callen chuckled. "Suppose we could make up for lost time?"

She laughed. "I guess we could."

In Love and War

Gregory Peake

War shouldn't exist, but when it starts, we must do what we can to end it.

At least, that's what my mother says.

My people have been at war for years. Our conflict spans the entire globe, but the violence, destruction and death is under the surface. Literally.

My name is Jilliandra and I am a sea dweller. We've had many names over the centuries—Sirens, Nereids, Oceanids, Dryads, Mermaids—but these all come from the surface. We've never had to label ourselves. We were too busy enjoying endless harmony.

That was, however, before the fighting.

Years ago, a huge land dweller's vessel dropped from the surface. We tried to help but there were no survivors, so we waited until the vessel reached the seabed. When it finally settled, we found drowned bodies and hundreds of crates on board. We were shocked to see that they were filled with plates, spear heads and various other sea dweller relics. We quickly realised that these dead land dwellers were scavengers, and they had packed their vessel too heavy with 'souvenirs' to safely navigate the sea.

I remember how quickly things turned. Almost immediately, everyone's attention turned to the relics, which represented hundreds of years of our proud history and were believed to be lost forever. It didn't take long for arguments to erupt. Some claimed the relics were family heirlooms, while others argued the relics were sacred to specific social groups. The fighting was almost inevitable. I had never seen reason go rotten so quickly. People went savage for a chance to stake their claim. They used rocks, coral and their bare hands to beat down anyone in their path.

My father was killed trying to protect me and my sisters, leaving my mother to pull us away as she screamed for him. I was young then, but I'll never forget looking back and seeing the red, chunky mist growing bigger and redder as the fighting and yelling continued. We spent the next few days huddled at home, crying for our father while armies formed.

The ocean has never been the same.

Fast forward to today. The war rages on and our side has taken drastic measures to ensure there are enough able-bodied sea dwellers to continue the fight. My mother, my sisters and I, and many other females of suitable age and fertility, are part of a breeding program to release as many eggs as possible. Every week, we are lined up to accept a queue of males who wrap their tales around ours, invoking us to release our eggs. Once we've expelled our eggs, the males then swim down to fertilise them.

It's a soulless, disgusting process. Breeding has never been about sexual pleasure, but it still used to involve a loving partner or at least a suitable mate. It once represented the creation of family and the growth of our people. In peaceful times it was celebrated, cherished and beautiful. Now I'm part of a soldier farm. I'll never get to meet my hatchlings or watch them grow. Nurses raise them until they are old enough to join the war effort.

What's worse are our males. I suppose the idea of fertilising so many eggs feeds their ego. The other females don't notice or care anymore, but the breeding program has become a grotesque competition of masculinity.

The men put on an act every time they swim up to me. I'm embarrassed for them. Some hold me by the waist or grab my breasts, 'for leverage' they say. Sometimes they perform water acrobatics, believing their show will entertain me and increase my egg count. None of this aids the process, and I roll my eyes every time.

Today is just like the others. I'm stationed in a designated space within a grid of females that spans the entire breeding site. Mother is in the section next to me.

As always, she's ready for the day, proud to be doing her part to win the war.

As always, the males are pathetic. They wear a smug superiority on their faces.

I'm currently facing one such loser. We stay entwined, motionless, until eventually he pulls away without a word. He leaves, flicking me in the face with his tail as he swims away.

That does it. "I'm going home early today," I announce.

"Come now Jilli, I know you have more than that in you," Mother says.

"What are you talking about? This isn't a sport. I'm not trying for a personal best here!"

"You could at least pretend to care about this. We're here to do our duty for the war. For your father."

"For Father? Are you serious? He was killed before the war even started. Don't bring him into this!"

I swim away before either of us say anything we might regret.

The weeks seem to be getting shorter as I swim to the breeding site. I take my place and stare blankly, waiting for today's first male to twist his tail around mine.

"Whoops, sorry, excuse me."

The words snap me out of my trance. There is a male in front of me, looking deeply uncomfortable. He seems to be struggling to find a comfortable position. His arms are out in front of him, as if he's unsure where to put them.

"Can I put my hands on your shoulders? I can put them anywhere… sorry… where would you prefer?" he stammers.

His politeness catches me off guard and I smile sympathetically. "You can put them on my shoulders if you want. You're the first one today so we won't be long."

He nods and rests his hands on me. "Thanks, it was either that or wave them around like I'm drowning, and that wouldn't make any sense," he says.

I smile again at his terrible joke.

In the few minutes we're entwined, I can't help but study him. His face is traditionally pointed and handsome and his arms and body are conventionally muscular—swimming through different pressures at different speeds gives most of our males lean, defined figures. What was unique, however, were the deep scars running across his chest. They looked new and serious. He must have been, or still be, in tremendous pain.

He releases his tail before I can ask him about his scars.

"Hope that was okay. Sorry for being weird. Enjoy the rest of your day," he says. He gives an awkward half wave and swims away.

Suddenly, nothing is more important to me than learning his story.

Another week passes and for the first time since the program started, I'm anxious to get to the breeding grounds.

I find my place in the grid. I can already see the pod of males waiting, but I can't spot the scarred male. My head drops in disappointment. Maybe he's in another section.

"Ah, the people you run into at breeding sites."

I look up, it's him! He swims closer and puts his hands on my shoulders again. It's only happened once before but it's already familiar and comforting.

"Well, as my mother says, we must do what we can to end the war," I say.

"Oh, your mother's here as well?"

"All in the name of victory," I reply sarcastically.

"So, how do the two of you make the day go by? Do you, I don't know, compete to see how many eggs you can manage—youth and beauty against age and... um... experience?"

I smile. His attempt to escape the situation he swam into is funnier than his awkward quip about my mother. I throw him a lifeline by changing the subject. "So, did you always want to be a fertiliser?"

He puts on a playfully disgusted look, "Ugh, don't call it that, this program is bad enough as it is."

"So, you're not a fan of the breeding program either?" I ask.

"Not particularly, but I was ordered to participate by my commander."

"Commander? You're a soldier? Were you fighting in the war? Is that how you got those scars?"

He opens his mouth, trying to find the right words. Instead, he looks down. "Oh, looks like we're done. Sorry, I better keep the line moving."

He starts to swim away but stops and turns, "I hope your day turns out okay. Don't let the grind get you down."

He bows his head and subtly curses himself under his breath, clearly regretting his parting words to me. For someone who has been through something so violent, he has very clumsy social skills.

How intriguing.

Another week goes by and I'm once again floating in my designated section at the breeding grounds. This time I haven't seen the scarred male and the day is almost over. I was hoping he would come back. I wanted to learn more about his injuries and why he's breeding when it clearly repulses him. He's interesting, which makes my day interesting... which makes my life a little more interesting.

I'm down to the final few males in my section. I drop my head with a mixture of exhaustion and disappointment.

Then I hear a familiar voice in the distance.

"Excuse me. Pardon. Sorry." The scarred male is pushing past the other males, making his way to the front of the line.

"Hey, what do you think you're doing?" one of the other males demands.

"Look, there's another female just one section over. I hear she's just started her shift so she's... ripe. Trust me, you'll look more impressive than you would working with the tired ones."

The males nod agreement and swim away. It's just me and the scarred male left.

"I'm so sorry, it's been a crazy day. I was put into another section so I came around again," he says.

I smile. "Ripe?

He grins sheepishly. "Trust me, I was shocked when it came out of my mouth. I was more shocked that it worked."

I laugh but immediately stop when he puts his hands on my shoulders. There's nothing funny about the way his touch feels. As soon as our tails connect, we start exchanging stories about our day. Neither of us had done anything interesting, but it doesn't matter. We're both happy to be talking.

He finishes a funny story about his childhood and I laugh so hard that it shatters our concentration. I look around and realise that the breeding grounds are empty. Everyone's gone and I'd stopped releasing eggs a while ago, but his hands have been gently grasping my shoulders the entire time. I don't want him to let go.

We both look around the empty space and there's an uncomfortable pause. Thankfully, he's the first one to speak.

"Looks like we've been left behind. It's getting late. Would you like me to swim you home?"

Of course I say yes.

I finally learn more about him. His name is Bokko, and he was indeed a soldier sent away to recover after being badly injured in battle. He was told that if he couldn't fight, then he could at least be useful by creating soldiers who could.

We agree to meet at the end of each day so Bokko stops coming to the breeding site. It's once again something I have to endure.

We spend hours every day talking, laughing and getting to know each other. He holds my hand as he fumbles through stories about his life. I tell him about Father and the toll his death had taken on my mother and sisters. Bokko holds me tight. Personally, I think he's always looking for a reason to hold me, but I don't complain. It makes me feel safe.

At the end of each day, before it gets too dark, we swim to the seabed and lie together on giant sea sponges. Sometimes we kiss passionately, sometimes we talk, and sometimes we do nothing but enjoy a peaceful, shared silence.

It's only been a few weeks, but I've never felt this way about someone before. My whole life has been engulfed in loss and war and servitude. Bokko has changed all of that for me, and I owe him the rest of my life. I want nothing more than to spend it with him.

Another day ends and we lie side by side on the soft sponge, watching fish and sea dwellers swim above us. I could live in this moment forever.

"Bokko, when do you think the war will be over?" I ask.

He runs his hands over his scars. "I don't know, but hopefully soon. If not, there'll be an entire generation who'll know nothing but war. I would hate that for my children."

"What about the hundreds of eggs you've fertilised?" I ask, tongue-in-cheek.

"Those aren't my children. They were coerced beings bred for war. No, when I have children, it'll be through the old ways. I'm going to love them and teach them and raise them with the perfect mate." He rolls onto his side and looks into my eyes. "Someone like you," he says.

I almost burst into tears. I've kept this to myself for as long as possible, but I can't hold it in any longer.

"I love you, Bokko."

He smiles. "I love—"

A shadow looms over us. I turn and see a massive figure swimming above. It heads towards us and as it gets closer, I can see the outline of a large male. His hulking frame is covered in armour. I look over at Bokko, his face falls at the sight.

"Who's that?" I ask.

Bokko doesn't answer. Instead, he gets up, looking guilty and defeated. I swim upright too as the large male approaches us.

"Can we help you?" I ask.

The male doesn't respond to me. It's as if I'm not here. A deep pit of anxiety grows in my stomach.

"I thought I had a few more days," Bokko says. His demeanour is different. The cute awkward male is gone, replaced by someone in authority—the kind that is earnt.

"I'm sorry, Captain, your convalescence is over, and I've been ordered to take you back to the front. Your men need you," the male says.

Captain?

The newcomer looks me up and down. "And if I may, sir, if you're healthy enough to keep this little thing entertained, then you must be in fighting form."

I swim forward to put the brute in his place, but Bokko stops me.

"Sargeant, that is out of line. Watch your tongue so I don't have to rip it out."

The male fearfully bows his head in apology, making it clear he doesn't believe Bokko's threat was empty. "I'll wait here while you say your goodbyes," he says.

Before I can speak, Bokko turns to me.

"Jilliandra, I have to go."

I try to keep my composure but start welling up. This is all so sudden. "Bokko, I don't understand. I thought you were out. I thought your wounds made you unfit!"

Bokko holds my hands in his. "I'm sorry Jilli. I honestly thought my injuries would get me out of the fighting, too. Ever since I met you, being by your side is all I want. These past few weeks... it's like the war isn't happening."

The dam inside me breaks and I cry as I stare into his eyes. His sad, longing face tells me everything I need to know: Duty calls.

My tears turn to sobs as I hug him around his neck.

"Please, don't go. I love you," I plead. "We can have the family you said you've always wanted. We can spend the rest of our lives together. Please, I love you!"

Bokko gently grabs me around the waist and kisses my lips. "If I make it back, there's no one else I would want to start a family with. I love you," he says softly.

Bokko releases his grip from my waist. His hands run all the way up my body to my shoulders, and then down my arms. He gently presses my fingers until, finally, he lets me go. The pain on his face is like mine, but he hides it better. Without another word, he swims away.

I hug my chest and weep even harder. I can't stop. I can barely concentrate on regulating my tail, which causes me to slowly sink like the vessel that started the war. I don't even realise when I hit the seabed. I close my eyes as I cry, hoping that he'll be back when I open them.

The weeks since Bokko left feel like years. There are no messages. For the first few days, all I did was cry. Couldn't he have refused the order to return? Couldn't he have pretended his injuries were still too severe? Was what we had, however brief, even real?

Did I mean anything to him?

I spend every day questioning whether our love should have been enough to make him stay.

I spend most of my time at home, staring at the door or out the window. I quit the breeding program, much to my mother's anguish. I can't bring myself to breed more soldiers. My sisters visit me occasionally, but without a similar emptiness in their heart they find it hard to empathise. Ironically, they all agree that the best way to help me is to focus on the breeding program, to ensure that there more soldiers out there to win the war. It makes me sick.

I'm preparing food, but for what meal I have no idea. Breakfast, dinner, they're all the same to me now. I hear a knock at the door and swim over to see who it is.

The hulking figure in my doorway is one I know. It's the muscular soldier who came for Bokko.

I don't invite him in. I don't say anything. I stay motionless, hoping that I'm strong enough for whatever he's about to say.

"Miss, I'm afraid I have some bad news," he finally says. "The captain ordered me to find you if anything happened to him. There was a battle… it claimed a lot of lives…"

My body goes numb. I can't move. I can't speak. All I can do is try and grasp the news as it smashes my heart like a battering ram.

"I'm very sorry. For what it's worth, he was emphatic about me finding you," the soldier continues. "I know it's no consolation, but during battle he found time to order me to come here. He didn't want to die with you thinking he didn't care. You meant a lot to him."

Too much information, too many questions, are running through my head. All I can manage to say is, "Was it quick?"

The soldier stares at me sympathetically. "It's best to focus on your memories of him, and that he was killed defending two wounded soldiers who were unable to retreat. He died a hero. I don't feel comfortable giving you the details of his end."

The soldier continues to offer his condolences but it's just noise to me. I stare past him until he realises I'm in shock, so he waits a small amount of time until swimming away. I can't hold it any longer. I burst into tears.

He wanted me to know. Even when facing death, he didn't want me to suffer. As I lie on the floor crying, I cling to the thought that the love we shared, however brief, clearly meant something to both of us. It's a thought that will give me strength to go on, or at the very least to get up off the floor.

Ubuntu

Linda Conlon

When Khaled found me as an unassuming young man, I lived in a hamlet that would eventually become Bristol. The modern world had only been counting its existence for nine-hundred and seventy-four years. I was nothing special and I'd never met anyone as exotic or fascinating as him.

He swept into the tavern where I worked like a torch illuminating a moor. All eyes turned to him. When his dark gaze bounced off every pair to land on mine, I caught my breath. He smiled, his cheeks dimpling and his eyes twinkling, and I felt a surge of desire flood my veins in a strike so vivid, I finally understood what those fumbling girls from the village had been trying to evoke when they snuck their hands down my pants.

He was in front of me in three swift strides and I blinked, uncertain I'd heard his footfalls on the grainy floorboards. My mouth snapped shut and I loudly swallowed the saliva pooling within. It was the only sound in the tavern besides the crackling fire as everyone waited to hear what this elegantly dressed foreigner would say.

"How are you named?" he asked, and I'd never heard a voice so akin to music. Truthfully, it took another swallow and a clearing of my throat to free my tongue enough to reply.

"I... be Heath of Wyndhame."

"Heath," he repeated in such a way as I'd never heard my name spoken, like a wish and an answer all at once. His lips curled into a secretive smile and my face flared with heat as he looked me over intently. "Are you indentured here?"

"I—in the tavern?" I queried, aghast to be stammering before such a fine creature but unable to find my ballast with his attention centred on me like a sunbeam.

He made an impatient noise, waving a dismissive hand towards the walls and the village beyond, which I'd called home since the summer I'd been borne, seventeen seasons before. "The tavern, a wife, children to feed, parents you care for. Any of it."

I'd grinned, finding his wording amusing and

giddy because I was beholden to none of those things. It felt like I'd passed a test. "No. None of that. I live freely."

"I am Khaled Salah Al-Tairi and I would have you do that by my side," he declared triumphantly and grasped my hand, a brow cocked questioningly. Dumbly, I'd nodded, and he whisked me out of the tavern and into the black night. It felt like my feet weren't touching the ground and I was exhilarated and terrified by what I'd agreed to.

I don't think I made contact with the earth again for years.

I learnt quickly what he was, for the rules of his existence were strict. No sunlight could touch his skin, or he would burn. No mortal food or drink could pass his lips, or he'd become ill. He needed blood to sustain him; blood from living creatures with a beating heart. He was stronger, faster, could hear thoughts and influence peoples' minds when he concentrated and he wouldn't expire except by extraordinary means. I shuddered and wept to think of him dead, picturing the things he described; his head cleaved from his body or his person set aflame. He cradled me and hummed reassurances as he wiped my tears, gentle with my sensibilities.

We travelled and explored the world by night, took shelter in dark places by day. My schedule adjusted to his and he was overjoyed to share everything with me. He talked as if he hadn't had anyone to listen to him for all his eight hundred years and I basked in his attention, his teachings. He'd travelled continents multiple times, criss-crossing regions whose languages he'd learnt, immersing himself in cultures, sampling lifestyles like a lord at a feast. He shared it all with me in detail so glorious I felt I'd been there.

Of course, I loved him. He didn't try to change me, but my edification was a natural consequence of being exposed to his stories, his life. I modelled myself on his graces, refined my appearance and accepted grooming advice in the hope of pleasing him. He complimented every new piece of clothing he provided for me, gushed about my fair hair turning from straw into shining curls with a regular bathing regimen and looked at me with such tenderness and raw admiration that I was suffused with the certainty I'd hung the moon purely to shine upon him.

The only frustration I had in that first year was his refusal to bed me or feed from me. He was determined to keep me pure, to develop our relationship as a savouring rather than a devouring. I watched his lips on the throats of others and burnt with jealousy. I watched them writhe against him and touch him wantonly and I hated them all with a strength equal to the burning of a thousand suns.

Khaled was patient with my spite, soothing me with eloquent descriptions of his irreverence for their behaviours, calming me with casual references to the many thousands of times he'd fed. I was bemused and impressed, gaining my first glimpse into the chasm that was an eternal life. The repetition. The confinement. The monotony. It occurred to me to look at the situation from his perspective, rather than imagining myself his victim and his lover, and I was humbled. Mortified, even.

"How do you bear it?" I asked, aghast.

As always, his smile was gentle. "Ubuntu," he said, before elaborating. "It is a belief from far south of my homeland. A way to look at the web of life. I am bonded to everyone; we all have our places and our roles. We are connected and dependent. I am because we are. As people have always been, so will they always be, as will I. There is no point in questioning it, or surging against it. Acceptance is revelation. There is peace in that."

It was the first time I remembered having a contrary feeling or thought towards him and I quashed it quickly. Acceptance was revelation, he said. I would have to wait for it to strike me. I loved him and I had every faith that he was right.

Things finally changed once we'd been together for thirteen moon cycles. I assured him I had matured enough, and he began to look at me contemplatively. My skin tingled when I caught those looks, even though he masked them with an easy smile and some enlightening conversation far removed from what I believed to be turning in his mind. I was restless with desire for him, unable to watch him feed without my pulse racing, my body yearning.

One night, he'd found a young man that had a bearing similar to his. He was beautiful, glistening and sinewy as his neck was pierced and his body throbbed in time with his offering. The pair of them were intoxicating, entwined like snakes as Khaled leant against a wall in the shadows of the building he'd lured his prey from. He clutched the man to him and I moved to his back, pressing into him as he ground against Khaled, my hands roving.

When Khaled realised what I was doing, his gaze widened in astonishment. I stilled, my heart in my throat, feeling pinned beneath his stare. He bit his tongue and pressed the bleeding muscle into the man's neck, sealing the holes his teeth had bored. The young man began to whimper, hoping for the delicious feelings to return, only to be unceremoniously thrust away from between us. Dazed, he staggered in a circle, trying to process what had happened.

"You are whole and happy. Return to your home," Khaled told him, and the man wandered into the night without looking back.

I heard him go, unable to look away from Khaled. The familiar tension of love stretched between us but it was taut, undulating on waves of lust. I thought I could see it reflected back at me but I was hesitant to move in case I ruined everything. I could barely hear anything over the blood rushing in my ears.

"Are you certain?" he asked me, his voice husky.

My entire being felt like it lightened and I could feel the smile I beamed at him stretching my whole face. "There is not a speck of hesitation in my body. I am certain. I love you, I want you. I want you to take me. I need you to."

At last, he acquiesced.

We established a new rhythm after that. Our bodies could unite and rest until repletion or exhaustion forced us to submit to sleep. Sometimes it was the sun, sapping Khaled of energy when it rose beyond the windowless walls of wherever we were ensconced. Sometimes it was my mortal body, every muscle quivering from exertion, my bones useless without their puppeteering.

I learnt how often he could drink from me, if he only took sparingly, resentful when he was forced to take from others to protect my life. I stopped going with him, unable to bear watching. He indulged my sourness when he returned, pandering to my petulance until I was reassured that I was his only true focus, the one he loved, his muse and passion. I was euphoric with my power, assuaged and content in our relationship.

Years passed in a haze of passionate devotion. We travelled consistently, foreign landscapes offering delights for my inexperienced eyes, his joy taken vicariously from mine. I met other vampires, unimpressed when they sneered and called me Khaled's 'pet', roused to indignation when they spoke condescendingly to my love and belittled his limited vampiric training. I was proud when he made a connection with an ancient that agreed to train him, rather than demean him, and his powers blossomed.

When I was twenty-two, I finally broached the subject of him siring me. He had no other fledglings and I was besotted, convinced I'd never survive without him in my life. I also didn't want to age beyond my youth, feeling he already looked younger than I and not wanting to appear incongruous to outsiders. The fewer questions we raised as a pairing, the smoother our life was.

It took months to convince him I was serious. He questioned my devotion, other vampire couples, his own motives. Eventually, he agreed and the deed was done.

I won't say it was a simple thing, because it wasn't, and it altered the trajectory of our relationship in ways I hadn't predicted.

The first axiom to fall was my concept of time. It had been rather fluid since I'd met Khaled but it became inconsequential after I was sired. There was night and hunting, learning to feed the gnawing hunger inside me without killing the fragile creatures in my grasp, understanding my new strengths and my altered limitations. There was finding the simplest of caresses staggering and climaxes to be sanity-shifting. There was day and recovery and suspension of everything until I awakened again the next dusk.

The second truth I embraced was one I had to keep to myself. Khaled founded his existence on his faith that he was an integral part of humanity, but I began to doubt that when I was now so much more than human. He was a tenacious romantic. Khaled had an ingenue's outlook on his existence and I loved him for it but I began to realise after just a few years that I couldn't share it.

He saw beauty everywhere, from the beating of a

moth's wings to the dance of moonlight on water. He forgave mortals their foibles and listened to nonsensical ramblings steeped in ignorance. These people that he drank from and indulged had nothing of value to offer him but he questioned them about their lives, as if it was of great consequence. He chastised my impatience, telling me that I wouldn't survive long if I didn't seek beauty around me. I scoffed. I had no time for such minutiae, there were vampire talents to learn, extraordinary skills to master, an untapped reservoir of power I needed to immerse myself in.

To his credit, Khaled was faithful to his creed and to me. To my eternal shame, I was not. Eventually, it broke me.

It took centuries. Dynasties rose and fell, borders were warred over and entire civilisations were irrevocably altered. Khaled and I were inseparable until I grew restless, and then we weren't. He was saddened by my rejection of his perspective and I hated myself for breaking his heart but I couldn't fight my nature and, true to his, he wouldn't insist I try.

We separated.

I pursued a life of vampiric development, surrounded by ancients that could do things I couldn't even imagine, awed by powers I couldn't immediately tap into. But I was patient and disciplined, devoted. I fuelled myself with blood from human cattle to attain the glory a mortal me from a millennium ago couldn't even have imagined. It happened, eventually.

I'm one of the most powerful in the coven, despite my lesser age and yet... it feels hollow. Without him to smile his dimpled pride at me. Without a reason to push forward. With no romance in my life.

I press buttons on a phone.

"Hello?"

His voice still has the ability to trickle down my spine like a caress and I'm filled with longing and regret. I imagine him holding the receiver, his head cocked just so, a little furrow of expectation narrowing his eyes as he listens for a response. I clear my throat to free my tongue, wishing I'd rehearsed what I was going to say rather than spontaneously trying to frame my mind to fill the cavity in me with his presence.

"Khaled. I... need to see you. To be with you. I miss you."

There's a smile in his voice when he replies and my soul sighs in relief. "Ubuntu," he says knowingly. "Come."

What She Wants

Delia Strange

Jade wants to go to the beach. I'd caught her daydreaming at the kitchen counter in the middle of making lunch and had a sneaky look. Impressions of sand beneath her toes, gulls wheeling overhead and the surf whispering and inviting. I steal away before she catches me, but she likely already knows I'm skulking around, delving into her mind for gift ideas as her birthday looms.

We're rare, but not as rare as you might think—mind readers. Mind reading isn't usually as clear as what I saw just now; that's a neat little trick I picked up because Jade's a mind reader too. It's better when mind readers partner up, even though I was told 'it never ends well'.

My mother liked Jade upon meeting her, but she threw me a look almost immediately afterward. I sensed her fear, and she likely sensed my confusion. She pulled me aside and whispered that warning, that it never ends well. I scoffed and told her I knew what I was getting myself into.

Bliss. Absolute bliss. That's what I was getting myself into.

Picture this: you have a partner who understands your mood, who says or does things that help you recover from being upset, or perhaps they give you the space you need without having to be asked. They just *get* you. They're perfect. You found your soul mate.

But it's more likely you found a mind reader.

Jade and I got married four years ago. We both want a kid, but we want to experience each other first. There's also no doubt our child will inherit our ability, and I'm a little intimidated at the idea of raising that. I certainly remember what it was like for me growing up. I was a 'freak' until I got the hang of it in my adolescence and then almost everyone found me 'charming'.

The next morning, I organise a picnic lunch and pack it in our little basket for two. Jade likes to sleep in, so I hope to be finished and hide it in the car boot. I'll suggest going for a drive and that's probably when my surprise won't be a surprise anymore because she'll want to know where we're going and will search inside my head for the answer.

It doesn't even get that far.

As I'm buckling the picnic basket closed, she wanders into the kitchen. She blinks blearily at me, looking cute in her short blue satin pyjamas and pretty in spite—or maybe because—of her bed hair. Her eyes flick to the picnic basket and back at me.

"Ethan. You looked."

She says it so deadpan that I don't know how to take it. Reading her is difficult in this case because she doesn't seem to know how to feel. There's a touch of appreciation at my gesture, but the main swirl is a mixture of disappointment, frustration, and sadness. I'm taken aback, and she sees the knowing in my face.

"Don't," she says, and I sense her embarrassment before I look down, ashamed.

"I wanted to surprise you."

"You can't," she says, half amused, half nonplussed.

"But you don't look as much as I do," I counter, and I don't have to scan her mind to know it was the wrong thing to say. "So, I can surprise you," I add in a meek voice that sounds defeated even to my own ears. I decide to lean into it and try to make her laugh. "Surprise," I say with a smile and show her my best jazz hands.

She scoffs but the answering smile on her face is a relief. I'm forgiven and we can move on. I decide to push my luck.

"Still want to go to the beach? Food's already

made." I sweep my arm over the basket like a gameshow model and she laughs. I bask in her laughter, letting it warm me up from the cold reception I received at the start.

"You goof," she says before skipping up to me and planting a peck on my lips. "What's inside?"

There's a strong urge to say it's a surprise, but I squash it down.

"Sandwiches."

"Ever the chef," she jokes.

It's been three months since the picnic—I don't want to say argument, but I don't know what to call it. A negative conversation, I guess. Since then, there have been more strange little negative conversations. They seem to be a version of the same thing. I don't even have to be properly delving into her mind, it can come from me just sensing her mood, or that she's feeling cold or thirsty. When I give her a hug at the right time or bring her a blanket or glass of water, she thanks me with a frown. Of course I peek to know how better to help her, because it's habitual and more accurate than asking her what's wrong. It's the same cocktail of emotions: appreciation, disappointment, frustration, sadness. The latter seems to be growing within her, and I don't know how to make it stop.

I bring her a bouquet of flowers when I come home after work. My smile is plastered on, and I go from room to room to find her. I'm about to head upstairs when I spot her through the glass doors sitting on a patio chair with a book. She's not reading, it's open but face down on her lap.

She turns her head to watch me open the glass door. I take two steps before I catch her thinking about insects flying into the house, so I turn back and slide it shut. Approaching her, I see a different expression on her face. It changed from a smile to something sour. My smile is long gone when I hand her the flowers.

"Could you just talk to me?" I plead.

"You make it so I don't have to," Jade says, placing the flowers atop her book. To her credit, she says this lightly, though the words themselves are snippy.

"That's not fair."

"It isn't?" she asks, the question strangely sincere. "You know exactly what to bring me, exactly when to hug me, exactly what to say. I never have to ask."

Why wouldn't she want these things? She and I had four perfect years until I made the picnic basket. How does a gesture so small, coming from a loving place, turn into this?

"You want me to… misunderstand you?" I stare at her uncomprehendingly. "I can't."

Jade's smile is sad. "I'm sure you can. You're doing it right now."

Standing over her while we have this conversation is uncomfortable, so I pull the other patio chair over. She waits me out as I sit and stare. There's a long silence that stretches as we look at one another.

I break it first. "What do you want?"

Her eyes go wide and she exhales in a way that

sounds like… laughter?

"That. Exactly that."

"What?" This conversation feels like falling in slow motion.

"You asked me what I wanted. Instead of looking. Instead of knowing."

I finally understand, and it horrifies me so deeply that I struggle to keep my expression in check.

"That would be like tying one arm behind my back. Worse! It would be like cutting that arm off."

She recoils. "You're that addicted to looking into people's minds?"

"Not all people's, not all the time. I hardly ever look, I sense." I gesture at her. "You must do it too. It's a passive ability."

Jade frowns, eyeing me with concern. "It's not passive. It's active. I have to open that part of my mind, even with sensing."

I realise how a mind-reader can be surprised. So surprised that they can even be shocked. I had no idea that she doesn't just leave that part of her mind open. No wonder my ability is stronger and more refined than hers. I've had more practise.

The worst part is, I've unwittingly kept this a secret from her for years. She's reacted so badly after noticing I always use it that I don't want to own up to the past. I didn't do it on purpose so it's not my fault. Why even bring it up? It'll just lead to more negative conversations, more despondency, more frustration. And, without knowing what's on her mind, I figure out what she wants.

"You want me to ask and not to look or sense. You want me to give you privacy."

I reach for her hands, the book and flowers on her lap making it awkward, but she meets me halfway and we link our fingers together. Tears run down her cheeks but her smile is wide, and I know I've provided the right answer. Look at me go, figuring the problem out without a scrap of mind-reading.

"Can you do that?" she asks. I hear her doubt, but I also feel it echoing in her thoughts. I don't think I could shut that part of myself if I tried.

And I don't want to try.

And how would she ever find out if she closes that part of her mind off all the time?

"I can." Because I don't want her to leave me, I add, "I will."

She starts sobbing so I help her to her feet, and she cries against my chest. The book and flowers fall to the floor but it's okay, she needs to be hugged right now.

We start having short, inane conversations that slows everything down. Instead of just giving her a blanket when I sense she's cold, I have to ask if she needs anything. Sometimes she doesn't realise, and I have to hold back and not give it to her. Ten minutes later she might figure it out and call me back to get her one. It's so tedious.

One day I'd slipped and just gave her a blanket. Jade took it with a thanks but then looked up at me suspiciously. I chuckled at her expression and told her she's always cold. She laughed softly in agreement and didn't give it another thought. I was worried she'd hear my heart thumping. I'll have to give her a blanket when she doesn't feel cold to hide my tracks.

She wants to go on a weekend retreat. I figure it'll be best to let her bring it up because I don't see how I can naturally guess.

We're watching television three weeks later and she still hasn't brought it up. I glance over a few times, enough for her to notice.

"Is something on my face?" The joke is light, playful. I want to keep this mood in our relationship because it's been really good again, like the early days, even with the tiny stain of deception. I don't mind slowing everything down so she can feel comfortable with me.

"Our anniversary is coming up," I say.

"It's a bit early to describe it as 'coming up'. It's three months away!"

"I'm trying to think of gifts, now that I'm not allowed to cheat," I smile but I don't like the way she's studying me. Is she reading me? My heart rate picks up.

"You don't know me well enough after almost five years?" The words are playful but don't match her expression, which is watchful.

"I'm just an ordinary husband now, which makes me clueless."

She laughs hard at that, throwing her head back on the cushion. She giggles intermittently as she gains control.

"Okay, clueless, the stereotypical gifts will work."

"You mean, chocolates, perfume, jewellery?" And against my better judgment, I add, "Raunchy weekend getaways?"

She presses her lips together and pulls them in like a naughty child who's been found out. Oh no, was she thinking about it as a gift for our anniversary?

"Or sexy lingerie," she suggests, her cheeks pinking and making her look more beautiful than ever.

"Does that count as a gift for you, though? Sounds like it's more for me."

"It can be both," she says coyly.

It's the Saturday before our anniversary and I get up and get dressed first while Jade sits up in bed reading her book. If she's not sleeping in, then she starts the morning off with a chapter. She must've read about a character wanting pancakes because she has them on her mind. I want to offer but I can't.

"We haven't used the waffle maker in a while. Want them for breakfast?" I give her a winning smile as she looks at me.

"That would be great," she says. She thinks I want waffles so didn't suggest anything else. Aw, I adore her. I head downstairs to the kitchen. It takes me about fifteen minutes to get everything ready and Jade arrives to give me a good morning peck on the cheek.

"Want to sit in front of the TV and watch news

entertainment?"

Jade hums in the affirmative, taking her coffee and plate of waffles to the lounge with her. I follow.

We watch TV for barely five minutes when she sets her plate down on the coffee table with a loud clink. I jump and stare at her as she runs her hands through her hair over and over, then storms to the centre of the room. I put my breakfast onto the table more gently than she did, and stand so I can look at her.

"What's wrong?" I ask, unable to make sense of the tempest of emotions in her. Something happened but there are so many feelings and thoughts battling each other that it's hard to pin down. I recognise the pattern enough from past relationships to know what it means. Her emotions are battling for supremacy. I won't be able to read her accurately because it's too blurry.

"I need to, go do…" She doesn't finish her sentence before she leaves the room.

I deduce that she needs space to process and hear her pacing upstairs. It's the first time I've come across her in such a state. Jade's usually calm, she rarely stresses out or panics. Did she forget to book the weekend away?

When she comes downstairs, there are thumps and bangs and I wonder what's going on. When I peer down the corridor, I see her with two suitcases.

She looks upset.

"What are you doing? Where are you going?"

"You're getting very good at that now, asking

questions you know the answers to," she seethes. The venom in her voice has me stepping back.

"Jade? Please," I beg.

"I know what you've been doing, Ethan. I looked."

My heart hammers in my chest. When did she look? Just now? What triggered it?

"I thought you didn't do that," I say. I don't like that it comes out caustically.

"And I thought you'd stopped. You lied to me!"

Lying is a big deal. We even wrote it in our wedding vows. A little joke, because we would always know the truth. Or so we'd thought. But I'd assumed it was about cheating, not about making us better.

"We could've had a perfect relationship, knowing what the other wants."

"It wouldn't have been real," Jade remarks, and I'm appalled.

"Knowing isn't faking. It's the opposite. If I knew what you wanted, I could get it for you. Or cheer you up when you needed it. You did it too."

Jade moves her head back and gives it a little shake, one of her hands clutching at a suitcase handle. "At the start, yes. When we were dating. And especially with your mother, so she would like me. But not when we got married, when I'd learnt about you enough to commit myself to you. I stopped. I would only open my senses when you were upset and when what I tried first didn't work. I knew you had your mind open more often, but I wrote it off as you being more emotionally ignorant and you needed the extra help."

"Emotionally ignorant?" I repeat, not liking the flavour of that particular insult. "I made things easier on us, bypassing words and going straight to the solution. I kept my senses open because I wanted to provide for your every need. Because I love you."

The tension runs out of Jade's body, her shoulders sag, her breath sighs, and her expression is unbearable.

Pity.

"Love me?" she asks softly. "You don't even know me. You reduced me to a combination of needs and wants, offering me the result and rewarding yourself with my reaction."

I struggle with her interpretation. It's so harsh. While she's not wrong, it's not how I think of her.

"You're more than that," I tell her.

"Yes, I know."

Words fail me when she advances. I briefly consider physically stopping her but then she gives me a filthy look so I don't. The suitcases clatter when she steps out onto the front walk. There's a car waiting. Jade must've called for one when she packed her suitcase. I dismissed the movements as pacing.

I'm so stupid. What made me think she would never find out?

"I love you!" I yell from the doorway when she closes the boot and heads for the passenger door. I see the tiniest of hesitations as she reaches for the handle, but then she gets in and the car drives away.

I know what she wants. And it isn't me.

ABOUT THE AUTHORS

JODIE LANE
Scifi Fantasy Adventure
JodieLane.com

M A MACLEAN
SciFi, Speculative, and
Fantasy for Kids, Teens and Adults
facebook.com/MartiiMacleanAuthor

MARGARET DAKIN
Murder Mysteries, Historical True Crime
goodreads.com/author/show
/6003764.Margaret_Dakin

NYSSA BASCHEL
Historical Fiction, Epic Fantasy Romance,
Urban/Mythological Fantasy
nyssabaschelauthor.com

J. H. NELSON
Contemporary Romance/New Adult
linktr.ee/J.H.Nelson_Author

RYAN ALCOCK
Action, SciFi, Fantasy, Speculative
facebook.com/RysBooks

R A PURTILL
Scifi, Fantasy, Speculative
facebook.com/PurtillWriter

FIONA EMILY
Romance, Paranormal, Fantasy
FionaEmily.com

A J R FRASER
Storyteller, Dreamer, Man of Mystery
—and maybe one day a Novelist

EVELYN CASTER
Urban & Paranormal Fantasy
linktr.ee/EvelynCasterAuthor

GREGORY PEAKE
Fantasy, Social Science Fiction, Dystopian,
Adventure, Thriller, Paranormal

LINDA CONLON
Scifi, Fantasy, Paranormal
WandererOfWorlds.com

DELIA STRANGE
Scifi, Speculative, Paranormal, Literary
DeliaStrange.com

Australian Pen Collection
#1 OBLIQUITY
#2 FUTUREVISION
#3 THE EVIL INSIDE US

An eclectic mix of short stories to a theme

From twisting turns and surprise endings, to predictions about the future both near and far, or exploring the flaws of the human condition, the Australian Pen collection will keep readers turning pages for each eclectic tale.

Find out more at
www.1231Publishing.com

www.ingramcontent.com/pod-product-compliance
Lightning Source LLC
Chambersburg PA
CBHW061452210726
48287CB00007B/2481